J   A#165909
LeMieux, A.C.   900 9/13/00

All the Answers!

G

{All The Answers}

√ ALL THE ANSWERS

Anne C. LeMieux

AN AVON **C** CAMELOT BOOK

AVON BOOKS, INC.
1350 Avenue of the Americas
New York, New York 10019

Library of Congress Cataloging in Publication Data:
LeMieux, A. C. (Anne Connelly)
All the answers / by Anne C. LeMieux.
p.   cm.
Summary: Failing algebra and being grounded for talking back to his father
are bad enough, but when he faces a beautiful new eighth grader and
her bullying twin brother, Jason is forced to take another look at his life.
[1. Fathers and sons—Fiction.   2. Schools—Fiction.   3. Conduct of life—
Fiction.]   I. Title.
PZ7.L537375A1   2000   99-27179
[Fic]—dc21   CIP

First Avon Camelot Printing: January 2000

CAMELOT TRADEMARK REG. U.S. PAT. OFF. AND IN OTHER COUNTRIES, MARCA
REGISTRADA, HECHO EN U.S.A.

Printed in the U.S.A.

FIRST EDITION

QPM   10   9   8   7   6   5   4   3   2   1

www.avonbooks.com

Dedicated with love to
my father John,
my husband Tim,
and always, my son Brendan

{All The Answers}

{Chapter¹}

A bad case of bed-head greets me in the mirror over my dresser. This morning it looks like a cross between a black rooster's plumage and a sloppy bird's nest. I need a serious glob of mousse to subdue it, but Pop's occupying the throne room. So I put on the pair of nearly clean blue jeans draped over my radiator and my Baaa-ad-To-The-Bone T-shirt, then switch on my computer. While it boots up, I stuff my feet into slightly used socks and work my way into my sneakers without untying the laces. Go to accessories, go to games.

Red on black, heart on spade, over a smooth, bright green field . . . Where's that jack of diamonds? Yess! Right here. The cards flip and slide across my monitor in just the right order, rolling the game along smooth and slick as new ball bearings. I've been an ace solitaire player since I was old enough to shuffle a deck. Pop got tired of playing Go Fish with me one day and taught me the game. But the computer deck beats a pack of Bicycles any day for efficiency and speed, plus the cascade when you win is really cool. This morning's first round is a winner with record bonus points for time, so I know it's going to be a fantastic day.

Solitaire—that's how I predict my luck on any given day. Some people read horoscopes; others call the psychic hotline. Me, I see what the computer deck turns up. The last time my luck meter registered this high, I scored twenty-six points in the Dexter vs. Rolling Hills holiday basketball tournament, winning the final game with a stunning last-second heave from midcourt.

On the other hand, the day I hit "Deal" thirty-seven times in a row and had to leave for school without chalking up a single win, my best friend Robbie Pellito spilled frog-flavored formaldehyde all over my brand-new Nike Air Jordans in science lab.

I hear the sound of water singing through our plumbing and a moment later, a pair of spit-shined wing tips shuffles to a stop in front of my open doorway. I watch my father in a tug-of-war tussle with his belt, as he tries to coax it a notch tighter. His spare tire, wrapped around the middle of his six-foot frame since he quit smoking last year, fights back.

It occurs to me that was about the time our relationship started changing. I mean, he's always been compulsively orderly, the type of guy who dots all his i's and crosses all his t's, a left-brain-dominant neatnik, whereas as I've always been more of the right-brainer, wing-it type. But lately he seems to be trying to force me into his mold. The result? Near-constant conflict. He changed from a dad who was more or less always on my side to a despot who's always against me.

Finally he gives up, slides his buckle to the "comfort margin" hole, and scowls. My quarters provide the perfect focus. I wait for the inevitable comment.

"This room," he announces, "would make the Augean stables look neater than a hospital supply closet."

I look around. The pile of clean laundry which I had fully intended to put away seems to have blended with wrinkled khakis, decaying sweat socks, and other sundry articles of dirty clothing. Like a textile lava flow, it obscures a good portion of the carpet. What little can be seen of the floor is covered with popcorn kernels, stray pepperoni pieces, pens, paper clips twisted into various artistic designs. My Chicago Bulls souvenir trash can is surrounded by paper wads that missed the Nerf basket attached to the wall above it.

My dresser's overflowing, as if my clothes tried to make a break from the drawers but were slain during the escape attempt. The dresser top looks like the aftermath of a SaveMart's meltdown. And there are about a dozen round spots of blue Stick'em-Up Putty on the wall, the posters having curled up, fallen down, and rolled under the bed for cover.

I don't have a strong rebuttal, so I give the standard response: a noncommittal shrug.

"Jason, this room is an absolute pigsty." Pop sounds pained. But he's tossed out a statement I can work with.

"Actually, Pop, that's a grave misconception. Pigs

are, by nature, very clean animals. And highly intelligent, too. People who have them as pets train them to use litter boxes and—"

"That's not my point!" His nostrils flare, and his eyes bug out a little. "I want this room clean before we have the Board of Health on our backs. In fact, I want it clean by tonight, or there *will* be consequences!"

Consequences. You wouldn't think a mere word could make every muscle in a person tense up. Well, except words like, "Halt! Who goes there?" or *"En garde!"* Maybe it's not as much the word as the way he says it, wielding it like some kind of sword, a parental power tool. To avoid escalating the skirmish, I will my muscles to relax and paste a smile on my face.

"Oops, look at the time," I say. "Gotta run, don't wanna be late. Punctuality's very important, you know."

In a most timely and helpful fashion, my mother's voice floats up the stairs.

"Jason, the bus'll be here any minute!"

Quickly I flip off all the computer switches, grab my backpack, and scoot past Pop. I can feel his glare burning through the back of my head like a laser as I hustle down the hall. Hightailing it down to the kitchen, I do a quick finger-comb along the way. Pop's wing tips clip the stairs behind me in stern, military mode. *Hut two hut two.*

My three-year-old brother Alex is in his booster chair, gnawing the top he's wrestled off the box of Cheerios. I point, and Mom lunges, substituting a banana for the soggy cardboard. He peels it, neatly sets the fruit down, and sinks his teeth into the skin.

"I need lunch money, Mom," I say.

While she rummages on the countertop, which is almost as disorganized as my bedroom, Pop's frown is deepening.

"And another thing, Jason, your mother is not an ATM."

"ATM. Hey, that could stand for Automatic Teller Mom." I try to joke it off, seeing him getting ready to spout the fiscal responsibility lecture. It's been over-played lately, like a monotonous radio song, ever since my father got bypassed for the promotion and raise he was expecting—make that, *counting on*—when the president of the venerable accounting firm of Kleeberg, Sander, and Roth plopped his wife's brother into the position.

"It's time you started showing some responsibility, young man."

Responsibility. Another simple word that's charged with negative connotations the instant it emerges from his mouth. Fortunately, the rumble of the school bus cuts him short. I grab the five spot Mom's pulled out of her purse and kiss her on the cheek. She shoves a package of Hostess donuts and a juice box into my hand. As I make for the door, I hear my father protest.

"Why does he get donuts while I get skim milk with these—pellets?"

"They're Grape-Nuts, dear, and he's a growing boy whose doctor hasn't advised him to watch his weight."

I can't help letting a snicker escape, for which Pop takes his revenge with one parting snipe.

"I want that room spotless by the time I get home tonight!" His mandate follows me out, but it doesn't

{5}

really dent my mood. No Grim Reaper of responsibility is going to put a crimp in my great card-karma day.

As the yellow bus rumbles up the road, Robbie, who lives three houses down, is doing his obstacle-course training. One leap down the four steps of his front porch, a dash across his yard, over the hedge hurdle. Then a sprint across Mr. Galemba's newly seeded dirt. One final broad jump over the low picket gate, and our paths converge on the curb at the SLOW CHILDREN sign.

Robbie jerks a thumb at the sign, panting and grinning. "Who's slow? That's gotta be a record."

The bus lurches to a stop, and the door burps open. We stumble down the aisle, and I slide in one of the few free seats left, right behind Amy Colter and her shadow, Debra Weinstein.

Amy had a thing for me a while back, end of sixth grade, beginning of seventh. I wouldn't call her my first love or anything, but you might say she was the other party involved in my first venture into guy/girl relationships. Once we went from being classmates who harassed each other in a friendly fashion to a more romantic involvement, something happened. Just being in the same room with her made me feel like I was wearing a too-small hat, a too-tight tie, and last year's shoes. Robbie observed that Amy had her claws in me but good; so I called the feeling "claws-trophobia."

Our brief fling ended during a seventh-grade field trip to the trash-to-energy plant, where she insisted on linking her arm through mine until I literally shook her loose. It wasn't my fault the shake-off hap-

pened to take place in the huge bay where the garbage trucks deposit their loads for processing. A
nicely stuffed Hefty trash bag cushioned the tumble
she took, then burst. Anyway, I apologized and all,
but it's still taken over a year to get back to a state
of guarded truce.

When Robbie asked me if the field was clear to
make a play for her a few months ago, I gave him
my blessing and a pair of earplugs. So far, his luck
hasn't been running too high. Although in my opin-
ion, he's luckier than he realizes.

"How's the weather?" I ask him once we're settled.
Computer-card karma is my thing. Robbie takes his
daily reading on the world by watching The Weather
Channel. I think he feels the more natural disasters
happening elsewhere in the world, the less likely disaster will score a direct hit on him.

"Wicked flooding in Texas," he reports. He leans
forward. "Hey, Amy, did you know floodwater flowing
at four miles an hour has the weight of one school
bus?"

"How much water?" Debra asks.

Robbie squints, what he always does when he's
thinking hard. "I forget," he says.

"Why would I possibly clutter my mind with a
stupid fact like that?" Amy says snidely over her
shoulder. I can see her rolling her eyes at Debra. "I
mean, who cares?"

Rob doesn't squelch that easily. "Well, probably
the people who used to live in the house that the flood
turned into an ark. They were up on the roof with
their eight cats."

"Oooh," Debra says sympathetically. "That's terrible! Were the kitties okay?"

"Yeah. Boat docked right to the chimney and rescued them all. Hey, Amy, did you know if the current's flowing at eight miles an hour, the same amount of water weighs as much as *five* school buses?"

Amy snorts delicately and ignores him.

"But how much water, Robbie?" Debra's brain tends to ride on a single track.

"I don't know how much," he repeats. "Just the same amount, that's all."

"Why not two school buses?" I ask Rob. "If it's only flowing twice as fast, why is it five? That doesn't make sense."

He shrugs. "Some kind of math thing, I guess."

Well, that explains it. Nothing about math makes sense to me.

"Answer:" I say. "Algebra."

Rob knows enough not to try and top me. "I give up. What's the question?"

"What's an undergarment worn by a well-endowed female aquatic microorganism?"

While I cackle at my own wit, Rob shakes his head. Debra's leaning over her seat now, giggling. Rob gives up on trying to attract Amy's attention and keys into Debra.

"You should have seen the news footage. There was this armadillo floating down the river on a tire."

"Was it alive?"

"I couldn't tell. It looked like a big, charred Cheerio in a river of chocolate milk though. Man, that water was muddy."

While Robbie continues to entertain Debra with the grisly details, I picture our bus as made of water, rolling along at four miles an hour. I imagine it filled with kids like a tankful of guppies, kind of a portable swimming pool. I puff my cheeks out, wondering if I could hold my breath long enough to make it from stop to stop, and I can almost hear water sloshing as we pull up at the last stop on the route.

And there, on the corner of Willow and Birch, a vision floats before my eyes. A female-type vision with corn-on-the-cob blond hair rippling down past her elbows, clothes in tropical shades of aqua, blue, and green: a form-hugging sweater, and a color-coordinated miniskirt, snug as a plum peel. Matching tights on long legs complete the ensemble. Maybe because of the ocean colors, the whole effect reminds me of a mermaid.

I slide my gaze back up to her face. Perfect features. Through the bus window, eyes greener than wet seaweed peer curiously into mine, twinkling at me. The corners of her mouth turn up in a charming grin. Then she puffs out her cheeks, and I realize I'm still holding my breath.

"Wooooooow!" Robbie stretches the word like a rubber band. "Who's that?"

"Ooooooof!" I reply, as he pokes me in the gut. I lean my head down between my knees, a little dizzy.

I'm enchanted. She twinkled her eyes at me! She grinned at me! She puffed her cheeks at me. I'm imagining her as a mermaid curled at the foot of a sand dune at the beach, crooning a siren song only I can hear, waves gently lapping, a full moon shining a path to eternal bliss across the water.

"Woooooow! Who's that?" Amy's voice is practically oozing, and it crosses my mind that it's strange Amy would gush over a girl.

A shadow falls across my vision as I look up.

And I'm doing a double take because my mermaid has suddenly turned into a mer-guy. Or what you might get if you crossed a mer-guy with a surfer-guru and some World Wrestling Federation hulk like the Beachboy Bomber. They must be twins. Same features, same fashion echelon, same green eyes, but this pair is glaring at me, like, oh, say, chunks of a plutonium and kryptonite alloy.

"Hey . . ." His voice is a not-unpleasant Southern drawl.

I think maybe I've mistaken shyness for hostility, or maybe the sun was in his eyes. Maybe he wants to introduce himself, or hey, even introduce his twin sister.

I reply, not unpleasantly, "Hey what?"

"Hey," he continues in the same mellow twang, "if I see you looking at my sister like that again, I'll use your Brillo-headed skull to scrub out every toilet bowl in school."

I hear Amy and Debra snickering. The mer-thug passes down the aisle. His sister pauses, shrugs apologetically, shoots me a token green-eyed twinkle and an impish smile, then also passes. And I suppose my embarrassment will pass. I think of what Pop always says about tax season: "This too shall pass—like a kidney stone."

This all takes a few moments to sink in. Brillo-headed? Toilet bowls?? *This* was *not* in the cards . . . .

{Chapter²}

"Philip H. J. Nevimore III." The way the mer-guy says it, it comes out Nevah-moah the Thuuuud.

I can see our math teacher, Mrs. Meehan, succumb to his surface charms just like half the female population of Dexter. They've been dropping like flies in a Raid shower all morning.

Mrs. Meehan looks like she could be the elderly proprietress of a thatched-roof tea shop deep in the English countryside. She's fairly hard of hearing, but her vision's sharp, and she can juggle numbers in her head so fast you can almost see circuits flashing in her blue eyes.

"And I'm Phelicia," I hear the siren say shyly. While her evil twin's voice hits my eardrums like the sound of a dentist's drill, hers is so smooth and soothing it could uncurdle cottage cheese. "That's P-H-E-L-I-C-I-A," she adds with a smile.

"Well, welcome to Dexter, both of you." Mrs. Meehan beams like a benevolent Mother Goose character, while I fumble for my daily excuse for not having the math homework. Sometimes she collects the assignments, sometimes not. Today, apparently, it will be not.

"All right, boys and girls, I'm going to pass back your tests, from which it is woefully apparent that there are some concepts you haven't grasped." Her voice warbles with grief at our misfortune.

She toddles over to her desk on her laced-up, high-heeled, old-lady shoes and picks up a thick stack of papers, which she gives to Debra to pass out.

"Philip and Phelicia, I'll give you copies. You don't need to worry about doing them—they're just so you can get an idea what we're studying."

While Debra scoots up and down the aisles, Mrs. Meehan hands blank tests to the twins and starts chalking problems on the board.

I can tell the grades kids have gotten by the expression on Debra's face. Colter's aced it again, and Mary Ellen Bobowick, too, no surprises there. Robbie's squeaked through, probably with his usual C minus.

My paper flops down on my desk, with so many red marks on it, it looks like it was corrected by a chain-saw-massacre victim. That would be an F. No surprise there either. I sigh and spot Mary Ellen in the next desk over, giving me a sympathetic look. Palms up, I shrug.

Mrs. Meehan has finished covering the board with hieroglyphics and turns to face the class.

"Since so many of you . . . ahem . . ."

She clears her throat delicately, as if she doesn't

want to hurt our feelings with a callous choice of words, like *are obviously morons, or would make a hamster look like Einstein—*

". . . did so poorly, we'll be doing this unit over and I will be giving a retest before the end of the marking period, which will give you an opportunity to pull up your grades." She looks over at Thud. "Philip, if you and your sister feel ready to take the test then, you may, or else—" Mrs. Meehan stops talking when he slides out of his seat, strolls up the aisle, and hands her the no-longer-blank paper. Less than ten minutes? He did the test in less than ten minutes?

After scanning it for a moment, her face scrunched into a frown of concentration, Mrs. Meehan tilts her head.

"Did you use a calculator, Philip? I don't allow calculators as a rule."

"No, ma'am," he drawls, and taps his head modestly. "This here's my calculator." Then he winks at her! This guy actually has the gall to wink at a teacher old enough to be his grandmother. Even worse, she falls for it!

She looks up at Thud like he's a Greek god who's just presented her with the gift of fire.

"My goodness . . ." she seems a little short of breath. "Perhaps—perhaps you should be in the gifted program, Philip."

Thud shakes his head with a disgustingly humble, hypocritically self-effacing smile. "My father prefers that I be mainstreamed."

Ahhh . . . I think. Mainstreamed, so you can make the rest of us look like mental midgets, to better reflect your glory. I can't help snorting, which Mrs. Meehan doesn't hear, but Mary Ellen does.

"Hey, want some extra help before the test?" she whispers kindly.

I smile grimly, but shake my head. "No thanks." I'd rather roll in molasses and dive into a fire-ant hill than voluntarily subject my brain to any additional math torture.

At lunchtime, Nevah-moah the Thud and his sister are together again. I've had to endure his presence in every single class this morning. Not only that, he guards Phelicia like he's her own private secret-service agent.

"Isn't there a poem about a croaking bird named Nevermore that showed up where he wasn't wanted and wouldn't go away?" I say.

" 'The Raven,' by Edgar Allan Poe," Justine Kelly informs me from the girls' table, next to ours. "And he said 'Nevermore.' That wasn't his name."

Right now Justine is unveiling her lunch. Her mother's a gourmet caterer, so while the rest of us have to eat cafeteria slop, she gets things like curried chicken salad in little croissants and tropical fruit cup with three-berry sauce. She sets aside what looks like a miniature cheesecake with pralines on top. I can't help but eyeball it covetously, and she catches me.

"Want it?" she offers.

"You're not going to eat it?" I say just out of politeness, pushing aside the congealed orange paste they call tomato bisque and reaching for the cheesecake as Justine shakes her head. I demolish it in two bites and she grins.

"Thanks," I mumble as my taste buds do an ecstatic little jig. "Anyhow, that poem reminds me of him." I jerk my head in Thud's direction. "Raven, huh? How about an eagle? He never takes his eagle eyes off his sister."

"Speaking of eyes, why don't you dig yours right out of your head and just *glue* them to her, Jason." Amy's eavesdropping from the next table. There's hostility in her tone. "P-h-elicia. Can you believe it, spelling her name with P-H? It's so cute it's nauseating."

"Yeah," Debra chimes in. "Gag me with a garden hoe. Why didn't they spell Philip 'F-I-lip' if they wanted it to match?" She wilts under Amy's glare, looking confused.

"Because that would be too much like what you say at a gas station, which would be *stupid* for a guy, Debra. Especially such a gorgeous guy." Amy's voice moves from metal to melted, going from she-twin to he-twin.

Mary Ellen starts to laugh.

"What's so funny?" Amy and I say with simultaneous indignation.

"You two. You're like fish."

Mary Ellen's our resident fish expert. She's got a humongous saltwater tank at her house with a bunch of tropical fish, all of which require more maintenance than a stock racing car owned by a lousy driver. My own experience with marine life is the goldfish I won at last year's school fair. I kept him in an old mayonnaise jar till he went belly up at the ripe old age of three weeks. It might have been pepperoni poisoning from the menu substitution I had to make when Alex ate my box of fish flakes.

"Ex-cuuuuuuse me?" Amy says now, looking down her nose at Bobowick.

Her attempt at a snub doesn't faze Mary Ellen, one of the few girls I know who has her head on pretty straight.

"It's a biological thing," Mary Ellen goes on. "You can't put two very similar species in the same tank. It's guaranteed automatic antagonism."

"Why?" I'm curious.

"Because if they're too much alike, they compete for all the same resources—the same food, the same territory in the tank, the same mate—"

"He's her *brother!*" I sputter. "He can't be her mate! Geez!"

"I'm talking about biological instincts, Jason," she goes on calmly, but her eyes are laughing. "And anyway, the fact that he's her brother activates another instinct—to protect the females of the pack from invaders who might pollute their gene pool."

"Pollute his gene pool? I resent that!" I say indignantly.

"So are you saying these two guys are biologically programmed to hate each other?" Robbie asks.

Mary Ellen nods. "It's a matter of survival. That's why fish and animals carve out territories—to have enough resources to survive."

"What does *that* have to do with *any*thing?" Amy asks. "Like *me*, for example?"

"It's simple." Mary Ellen shrugs. "You and Jason have both had your social territory invaded by foreign but similar fish. And you're reacting the same way the parrot fish and the anthias did when I made the mistake of putting them in the same tank."

"So what happened?" Robbie wants to know.

"They were both about the same size and color, kind of coral pink. The parrot fish wouldn't let the anthias near the food flakes. He kept chasing it down into the caves. Every chance he got, he charged it. Intimidation."

"And?" I'm trying to picture me charging the Thud in the lunch line to keep him away from a bag of potato chips.

"Finally the anthias turned against itself and started charging the side of the tank." Mary Ellen shakes her head.

"Not . . ." I say.

"Yep. Bullied to death. Just couldn't take the harassment. It was really sad."

This could be more serious than I thought!

"I wonder which fish Jason is," Amy says now.

"Is that P-H-ish?" Robbie cracks up.

I look over at the twins. They're sitting across from each other, heads together, looking tighter than the knots in my old sneaker laces. It's kind of amazing that two such similar people can spark such polar responses in me and Amy. Maybe Bobowick is right. Thud sees me staring at them, stands, and casually strolls over. All the hairs on the back of my neck feel like they need de-electrifying with a hit of Static Guard spray.

"Hi, Philip," Amy coos. He gives her a pleasant nod, then picks up the apple from my tray, and tosses it in his hand. I hear Robbie suck in his breath as I feel an influx of righteous rage. The Thud just commandeered part of my territorial nutritional resources!

"You wanna put that down?" I say. Every muscle in my body is poised to spring like a crossbow. Well, maybe not a crossbow . . . maybe more like a beach ball on a sea lion's snout.

"Sure," he drawls. He drops the apple back on my tray. Well, not exactly on my tray. To be precise, he drops it in my half-eaten bowl of tomato bisque. Gummy orange cracker muck spurts all over my T-shirt.

Stunned, I look down, a distant part of my brain noticing that the stain resembles a vandalized jack-o'-lantern. He walks away.

"Whhooooo." Robbie exhales. "Hey Jason, it looks like this is going to be a real Darwin thing."

"Huh?"

"You know—'Survival of the P-H-ittest'?" He cackles in spite of his sympathy.

I thought my luck was all lined up today. Could the cards have played me false?

"So whadaya think?" I ask Rob after school. We're at Maple Hill Elementary shooting hoops. I dribble a few figure eights between my legs, then go in for a lazy over-the-shoulder shot.

"What do I think of what?" Rob asks. "Ooof." He falls back a step as I pass him the ball. Rob's on the skinny side, the kind of kid who could hide behind a fence post if he stood sideways. He shoots from center court, and the ball bobbles around the rim, then drops off the side. Lack of athletic aptitude's never fazed him much. Nothing really seems to bother Rob, in fact. It's like he was born with this built-in insulation, a protective bubble that filters out anything that might seriously rock his apple cart. It's a quality that makes him pleasant to hang around.

"About the Nevi-mo-ahs," I say casually, and make a fast left break around an imaginary opponent for a lightning-fast layup. While Rob scratches his stomach and considers his response, I court the ball, then do it again, three times in a row. *He shoots, he scores!* the announcer in my head yelps with admiration. My left-handed layups are a specialty that have given me an edge in more than a few games. I bounce the ball to Rob, and he dribbles in place.

"I think they're both going to have an impact on the climate around here," he says finally.

I raise an eyebrow.

I'm not ready to reveal how smitten I am with Phelicia, so I don't ask him for further explanations.

{Chapter³}

Mom's in the kitchen gluing flower petals to fat candles when I get home from the courts. She's an artsy-craftsy person, specializing in homemade seasonal ornamental accents for the home, that she sells at, what else, arts and crafts fairs. She used to have a mail-order business, but shut it down when Alex was born because it took too much time. On the table, next to sheets of pink cellophane, there's a page of labels, an ink pad, and her signature stamp, *Margaret Hodges.*

Alex is in his booster chair with a coloring book and a set of oversize crayons. The marks he's made on the page resemble my algebra test, but at the moment he's not coloring, he's trying to stand the crayons up on the table like a battalion of small soldiers. Every time one falls, he knocks them all down and starts over.

As Mom wraps one of the candles in the cellophane, she shoots me an unhappy glance. "I'm very disappointed in you, Jason."

"What? Why?" Where is this coming from?

She presses her lips together and gives me another look. "I'm afraid I can't help you talk your way out of this one, and when your father gets home from work, we're going to be having a *Serious Discussion*."

"What's the matter?" I ask, trying to sound innocent. She just shakes her head sadly, not answering.

I wonder when they're going to spring it on me. Even more, I wonder what "it" is. The rest of the afternoon, I sense it in the air, sense it coming, sure as death and taxes. Tax season, by the way, is another reason Pop is strung tighter than a barbed-wire fence and twice as prickly right now. It's only a little more than a month before every certified public accountant's nightmare day, April 15.

The impending *Serious Discussion* floats over the dinner table, over the broiled scrod, boiled potatoes, and soggy spinach—the typical bland, healthy dinner that my mother's been serving ever since Pop's checkup last month. He came home and reported his blood pressure was in orbit, his cholesterol level rivaled Reggie Jackson's batting average in his best year, and the doc told him he had to drop twenty pounds.

"I quit smoking to salvage my cardiovascular system," he mutters grumpily now. "What happens? I gain twenty-five pounds. And what does that do? Threatens my cardiovascular system. What am I supposed to do, quit eating?" Glancing down at his plate, he appears to weigh that option carefully. Then he snorts sadly. "Why don't I just quit breathing? That'd save wear and tear on every system in my body."

Normally, I'd make some kind of response, but my

instinct for self-preservation cautions against it. My mother doesn't say anything either. Throughout dinner, she keeps glancing back and forth between me and my father, looking more distressed with each passing minute. I still don't know what the problem is, but I can't help feeling guilty for causing my mother discomfort of mind or heart.

I mash my meal together, in an attempt to make it look like I consumed at least some of it. The results appear so unappetizing that a starving hound wouldn't give the plate a second sniff. No parents with any kind of compassion could possibly force their offspring to ingest it.

"May I be excused?" I mumble it as a formality, since I'm already pushing my chair back, charting my exit. I'm starving, but I'll fill up on donuts later. Picking up my plate and Pop's empty one, I carry them to the counter and take three steps toward the doorway. But it's a no-go. Pop's in instant authority mode.

"Where do you think you're going, young man?"

"Where do I think I'm going?" I pause as if for serious consideration, "I think I'm going upstairs," I say innocently. "To do my homework."

"Ah . . ." He nods, stroking his chin. "Margaret, Jason thinks he's going upstairs to do his homework. Homework . . . maybe that's something we should talk about . . ." His tone has gone from stern to deceptively conversational. Not a good sign.

I take another step toward the doorway. "Well, you know, I don't want to be one of those 'All talk, no action' guys, so talking really isn't necessary—"

"*SIT!*" he barks, and points to my chair.

"On the other hand, if you want to talk, we could

do that," I say, and saunter back to the table. I'm racking my brain, still wondering what the heck I did to stir up this much of a wasps' nest.

Mom's cleared the rest of the table nervously, and now she sponges a spot in front of Pop. Pop reaches behind him and grabs a manila envelope from the kitchen desk. While Mom wipes down Alex, who's wearing most of his dinner, Pop opens the flap and pulls out a thin stack of familiar-looking documents, short, typewritten notes on my mother's preprinted, floral-border computer stationery. With a familiar stamped signature: *Margaret Hodges*. Uh-oh. I swallow. The topic for the *Serious Discussion* is becoming uncomfortably clear.

Pop motions to Mom to join us, clears his throat, and starts to read from a Dexter Junior High memo on top of the pile.

"Dear Mr. and Mrs. Hodges,

Enclosed are several notes which your son Jason has presented recently in lieu of homework assignments. I thought you might like to have them back to keep among your personal papers, should you ever decide to write your memoirs. Raising a son like Jason no doubt will provide enough material for several volumes. In the event, however, that they did not actually originate with you, I wanted to share them, evidencing as they do such a high degree of creativity. Some, indeed, may even be suitable for framing, as examples of the most extraordinary excuses for lack of homework tendered to me during my forty-year tenure as a teacher of eighth-grade mathematics.

Unfortunately, entertaining as they are, they will not suffice to satisfy the academic requirements for this class.

Unless all assignments are made up within two weeks, and current assignments are handed in on time, I will have no choice but to reward Jason with a failing grade for this marking period.

Best regards,
Mrs. Estelle Meehan"

I'm flabbergasted! Mrs. Meehan, the soft touch of teachers, ratted me out! Not only that, she did it with indisputable, hard evidence. And who would have thought that such scathing sarcasm could lurk inside such a sweet-little-old-lady head?

Pop is perusing each note in silence, but an egg-plant-colored flush is beginning to rise from inside his white collar, ominous as the rumble in the belly of a volcano. After a minute, he begins reading out loud.

"Dear Mrs. Meehan,
   Please excuse Jason for not having his math home-work today. He did it on recycled loose-leaf of an inferior grade and it disintegrated.
   Sincerely,
   Margaret Hodges

Dear Mrs. Meehan,
   Please excuse Jason for not having his math home-work today. He was assisting me with some domestic main-tenance of the Hoovering kind, and we experienced a major power surge. A SaveMart sale flyer also succumbed.
   Sincerely,
   Margaret Hodges

Dear Mrs. Meehan,

Please excuse Jason for not having his math home-work today. He did it so fast, the friction of his pencil ignited the paper and it burned up.

Sincerely,

Margaret Hodges"

Now he's leafing rapidly through the rest, muttering.

" . . . 'assures me he did it in study hall yesterday, but on the way home from school, he was mugged by a roving gang of mathematically deprived youthful thugs? . . . spontaneous combustion? . . . his brother Alex suffered a bout of his chronic pica and ATE IT!!??' " He glares at me.

"Well, it could have happened," I say weakly, recognizing a shoddy defense, though pica is an actual medical thing, when little kids chow down on nonfood items like mucilage and dirt and chalk. We found out about it when my parents had to confiscate Alex's blankie after they discovered why it was shrinking: He was eating it, thread by thread.

"Jason, how could you?" My mother interjects reproachfully. "The doctor said Alex's . . . habit . . . is *not* pica. But in any case, it's nothing to joke about." The look she gives me makes me feel lower than a worm's belly button.

Pop waves the papers. "Do you have anything to say for yourself?"

I clear my throat.

"Well?" It seems he expects some sort of verbal response.

"Uh, early April Fool? Heh-heh?" I force a tiny chuckle.

Pop's eyebrows draw together so fiercely, they look like a small brown bat perched just above his glasses.

"Well I have a few things to say. Allow me to ENUMERATE."

As if I could stop him, I think, suppressing a sigh. My plan for math-homework avoidance, which I thought brilliant, seems to have backfired.

"Number one, it is a crime to forge the signature of another person."

"I didn't forge it, I stamped it," I point out, to keep things in some kind of perspective.

"That is irrelevant," he says through gritted teeth. "The criminal intent was the same. Number two, you are clearly not doing your required assignments, which in MY book"—he waves the papers—"is a serious offense. Number three, the assignments happen to be in mathematics, which makes it a CAPITAL offense!"

"Look, Pop, just because you and everyone in your family has always been a genius in math doesn't mean I got those genes," I say. I know I'm skating on paper-thin ice, but the only other option is to cave in, plead completely guilty, and throw myself at the mercy of the court. A rod of resistance inside won't let me, and the louder Pop gets, the stronger it gets.

"THAT IS BESIDE THE POINT!" he thunders.

The vein in his left temple is throbbing like a Mexican jumping bean. Remembering his blood pressure, I force my attitude to retreat a few paces, not wanting patricide from a fatal dose of back talk on my conscience.

Well I have a few points I'd like to *ENUMERATE*, too, I think, prudently keeping my thoughts locked inside my head.

Number one, I hate math, and I always have. English? Fine. History? No problem. Science? Great scope for creativity, especially in lab. But math? It turns my brain to sludge.

Number two, I have better and less painful things to do than math homework, like sticking sharpened bamboo shoots under my fingernails or doing the Curly shuffle on a bed of broken glass.

And number three, when we started the unit on algebra a few weeks ago, my brain hit a brick wall, plain and simple. It said to me, "Jason, give it up. A smart guy knows his limits—here's one for you: algebra." I mean, it's not even just numbers. They start mixing in letters and powers and all kinds of numbo-jumbo. My eyes take it in, trot the equations upstairs. Every lobe in my brain goes into spasms. We're talking DNC. Does not compute.

Pop seems calmer now. He picks up the papers again, shakes his head, and tosses the pile on the table. Then he takes off his glasses, scrunches his face up as if in pain. Finally, he rubs his eyes as if he's trying to erase what he's just seen.

"Go to your room," he says evenly. "Do your homework. *ALL* of it. We'll talk about this further tomorrow."

I slink away. At least this new crisis has distracted Pop from resurrecting the issue of my personal domestic habits.

"And while you're up there, *clean that room!*"
What is the man, a mind reader? Still, all things considered, I feel like I've emerged from this battle relatively unscathed and let loose a sigh of relief.

As I'm leaving, I hear him say to Mom, "I am going to expire of terminal taste-bud atrophy if you don't go back to your regular cooking, Margaret."

Upstairs, after a few—well, okay, two dozen—games of solitaire, I've calmed down sufficiently to consider the possibility that I might want to rethink the situation. I have zero interest in going to summer school, not to mention being excluded from graduation, which suddenly seems a prospect real enough to make me sweat a little. With a sigh, I open to tonight's math assignment, questions at the end of the chapter on so-called simple equations. Problems 11–15, which fall under the heading, "For Fun," some grown-up math nerd's idea of cute.

I read the first one. "A hungry fox ate 225 grapes in six hours, each hour eating 15 more grapes than during the hour before. How many grapes did he eat in each of the six hours?" I stare at it, and read it again. Huh? They've got to be kidding. For starters, I'm not at all convinced foxes eat grapes, and if the authors of this textbook would mislead me about something like that, why should I entrust my mind to them for anything?

I shake my head, and go on to the next problem. "A visitor to Farmer John's chicken coop asked him how many chickens he had. Farmer John replied, 'If ¼, ⅕, and ⅙ of my flock of chickens were added together, that would make 37.' How many chickens does Farmer John have?"

I feel my brain twisting into contortions that can't be healthy. I have absolutely no clue how many chickens the geek farmer has, nor do I care. Furthermore, I think Farmer John should get a good smack upside the head for giving such a convoluted answer to his visitor's sincere, straightforward question. Finally, I'm getting pretty steamed that anyone should suggest I waste my valuable time on this earth trying to figure it out. I grab a piece of paper and dash out an answer that should cover both problems.

"If the hungry fox from problem 11 survives the effects of pigging out on that many grapes, he can trot over to problem 12 to good old Farmer John's for his second course—I'd suggest the chicken—and then nobody will have to injure their gray matter pondering such absolutely useless and ridiculous questions."

"For Fun," the book says. I'd like to know what the weirdos who write math textbooks do when they really want a laugh riot—go to the emergency room and have their stomachs pumped?

{Chapter⁴}

I wake up the next morning out of a dream that would win an Academy Award if I were voting.

March Madness, the NCAA playoffs, I was first-string point guard for the perennial contenders, the North Carolina Tarheels. Final seconds of the last quarter of the seventh game of the finals, score tied at 79. The cheerleaders, led by none other than the P-H-abulous Phelicia, going wild on the sidelines. The ball coming downcourt, the pass to me, two seconds left on the clock.

"Go for it, Jason!" The imploring siren voice over the roar of the crowd. A mighty leap, a gorgeous arc, through the hoop, a three-pointer to win the game! The thunderous sound of victory! A joyous cartwheel by the head cheerleader, straight into my arms! Both of us hoisted by the team and carried out on their shoulders. And who was on the sidelines right behind the team bench, madly waving a pennant? None other

than my father, finally come around to recognizing my greatness. With a joyful grin on his face, he gives me a double thumbs-up.

Funny, that image stays with me more than the hug from Phelicia. I lie in bed for a few minutes, awake but with my eyes closed. I think it came up from some archives buried deep in my memory. I let my mind wander, and suddenly, the real memory is there, that double thumbs-up, that grin: the first time I ever scored in peewee basketball when I was seven years old. Pop was my team's assistant coach, a semi–drill sergeant kind of guy even then. I was always afraid I'd be a disappointment to him. My mind wanders further back, Pop climbing down from a ladder, having just put my first basketball hoop on the garage, nine feet, one foot lower than regulation, so I'd have a chance of actually making a basket, then showing me how to go in for a layup. Where did all that go? I sigh, and get out of bed.

Down in the kitchen there's a curiously relaxed atmosphere. Mom's alone sipping coffee and reading a crafts catalog.

"Where is he?" I ask cautiously.

"Which he?" she asks in a neutral tone, and I frown slightly because I know she knows I'm not referring to Alex, and there's only one other he who lives here. My mother and I have always been on the same wavelength, understanding what the other is thinking without the need for a lot of words. Her question makes me feel like she's blocking our special channel of nonverbal communication. I'm not sure why.

"The Tyrant of Tense," I say.

She refuses to smile. Instead, she looks at me seriously. *"Your father,"* she emphasizes the words reproachfully, "went to work early this morning. You know, he's in a very difficult situation right now, Jason, under tremendous stress. I'm asking you, please: Don't add to it." She goes back to browsing her catalog.

A barb of guilt stings me, and my head actually hangs a little of its own accord. I go about the rest of my morning business, restoring my equilibrium by musing on the Phelicia part of my award-winning dream.

Breakfast eaten, special attention paid to de-Brilloing my hair, I'm heading for the door ten minutes early, when Mom hands me a note along with my lunch money.

Uh-oh. "Is this for Mrs. Meehan?"

She shakes her head. "It's for you. From your father."

I'm stopped in my tracks. Do I really want to start my day like this? I think perhaps not.

"Thanks," I say, and pocket the paper along with the money.

Mom raises her eyebrows at me. I look away and make my escape. But outside as I stroll to the bus stop, my curiosity gets the better of me. Hey, maybe it's not a paternal subpoena. Maybe it's even a note of apology for him having been such a humorless crank about the whole math magilla. I pull it out, unfold it, and below MEMO FROM THE DESK OF JOHN HODGES, read the few curt words my father penned for me:

What? No salutation? What kind of a letter is this to send to your firstborn son? Not a lot of scope for any broad interpretation, unless I want to speculate on what he means by "or else." I have to say, the tone of it tees me off extremely. I wad it up and throw it in the gutter, thinking about how radically this father-son relationship has deteriorated. Upon slight reconsideration, I retrieve it, gritting my teeth. No need to litter, plus if Pop should happen to spot it when he comes home, my disposal of his memo could add fuel to the fire.

Rob sprints over just as the bus pulls up. We take a seat behind Amy and Debra again. The two of them have their heads together, and Amy's flipping the pages of a magazine. I lean over the back of their seat.

"Watcha got?"

"Back off, Donut-Breath," Amy says. "It's the spring issue of the literary magazine. Hot off the press." She closes it briefly so I can see the cover.

It seems to me the editor in chief's name is a little more prominent than it needs to be, but I don't bother to comment. Having myself submitted a short piece of prose for publication, I'm eager to see my own name and humble words in print. I snatch it up and sit back in my seat.

In half a heartbeat, Amy's poking her claws at me. "Give it back! You'll get your copy in homeroom."

But I curl myself up like a porcupine while I peruse the table of contents. Let's see, out of the two dozen items listed, I count five poems with titles too sappy to bear repetition by, well whadaya know, our very own editor in chief. The rest are assorted titles by Dexter's literary wanna-bes. Something seems to be missing, though, my brief essay called, "Manifesto of the Manifold Magnificent Qualities of Men."

Amy manages to grab the magazine back, ripping a corner of the cover in the process.

"Look what you did, you idiot!"

I ignore the shrillness in her tone and glare at her. "Where's my essay?"

"Essay-shmessay," she snaps, sliding back into her seat.

"Geez, what a poet," I say loudly. "Better write that one down, Colter, it's a classic. Hey, make sure it's the first poem in the next issue."

"Well it's a lot better than what *you* wrote," she

says. "Your so-called essay was the most arrogant, macho pile of manure I've ever read."

"Oh yeah?" I'm stung, but don't want to show it. "Who are you, the Queen of Literature?"

"No, just the editor in chief of *Dexterity*." Her smug expression cries out for a chocolate cream pie in the face, but unfortunately I don't happen to have one handy.

"It's Colter's revenge," I grumble to Robbie. "Hell has no fury like a woman scorned."

"Huh?" Rob says pleasantly.

"Never mind." I sigh. Rob's a great guy, but he's more into video games than quotes from classical literature.

"How were the cards this morning?" Robbie asks skeptically, matching my snail's pace as I haul my maimed and bruised body back to the locker room after phys ed.

"Don't ask," I mutter.

With every clang of a locker door jangling my shot nerves, I collapse on one of the short, narrow benches. My sweat-soaked shorts and T-shirt laminate me to the wood, and I'm certain I'll never move again. I fold my hands over my chest, linking my fingers together so if my arms fall right out of my shoulder sockets, they won't litter the floor.

Robbie's looking concerned. "Man, Thud was all over you like a bad rash out there."

I'm still too winded to give voice to any of the murderous thoughts my battered brain is managing to hiccup forth. Turns out Thud's not a surfer-guru after all. He's—what a coincidence, just happens to be *my* position—a point guard, oh yes, first-string All-State. His average last season at his old school, a stat he just happened to drop, was twenty-two points a game.

"We take you now to sports highlights for Dexter Junior High's third period gym class scrimmage: Captain Jason Hodges, formerly the uncontested star of the Dexter team, was no match for the burly Texan newcomer. Thud dismantled the opposing squad's defense with an arsenal of questionable but effective tactics, prompting Coach Matthews to dub the losers 'A Hodgepodge gaggle of brainless, gutless geese.' When it was pointed out to the coach that the correct term would be ganders, he displayed an unsportsmanlike lack of gratitude for the information.

The kicker occurred near the end of the last period, right when the girls were trotting in from the field, when Hodges, in an ill-fated attempt to impress Phelicia—she of the limpid girlish giggle that would have hit his eardrum like a caress were the occasion for it anything other than his utter defeat—went up for a rebound, and was low-bridged by Thud. The former star's knees buckled beneath him, and he went skidding so hard across the court, he left butt-shaped tread marks."

"Answer:" I mumble. "Thud."

"I give up," Robbie obliges.

"What's the sound of my body hitting the gym floor after being charged by that cretin? I can't believe Coach called the foul on me."

"Hey, Jas, it could be worse." Robbie nudges my arm with his knee and I wince.

"How?"

"Well . . ." His brain has to stretch for this one. "Well, you could be living in Sri Lanka, with the roof blown off your hut by a monsoon, and all your stuff getting soggy."

I manage to push one lid open long enough to give him an extremely hairy eyeball. I know he's trying to make me feel better. It's not working.

"Hey, if I put a lily in your fist, you'd look just like a corpse, you know that?" he observes now.

"Then please go away and let me rest in peace," I say.

I can tell he's nodding sympathetically. Then I hear his sneakers squeak across the linoleum as he heads for the showers.

"You look like you tried to fight your way out of a paper bag and the bag won," Mary Ellen observes as I drop into the seat directly behind her and plop my lunch tray on the table.

A weary snort is the best response I can come up with.

"Bad day, huh?" Justine says sympathetically.

Bad day? My own father leaves me a threatening note. My literary ambitions are quashed by a militant-feminist, power-mongering editor. Math class first period, Mrs. Meehan hits us with a surprise pop quiz, after which I'm forced to witness the disgusting spectacle of Thud the Human Calculator explaining all the right answers to the class. Then I'm mugged right in my own school by Thud the Basketball Thug. And it's only noon.

"Let's just say the kind of day I've been having

would make a barefoot walk over burning coals look refreshing." I attempt a smile, but it hurts too much.

Happening to notice the sliced ham and Swiss and fancy lettuce on miniature pumpernickel sandwiches that Justine's unwrapping, I quickly force my eyes away, lest an unattractive fountain of drool suddenly spring from a corner of my mouth. I pick up my soggy taco, decide it's not worth the effort of biting and chewing, and I drop it on my tray.

"What happened?" Mary Ellen asked curiously.

"Well, to start off, my father happened—happened to let me know that if I don't clean my room today, I can expect dire consequences."

"What's that mean?" Rob asks. He picks up my taco. "You gonna eat this?"

I shake my head. "It's all yours if you're in a risk-taking mood. And I don't know what it means. We've had run-ins before, but the whole deal seems to be escalating toward full-scale war these days."

"Why don't you just clean your room?" Justine says. "Wouldn't that be the easiest thing to do?"

"Because," I say, "it's *my* room. It's *my* turf. It's the principle of the thing." Thinking about it gets me mad all over again, and I resolve that whatever "or else" means, I'm not going to fold. I'm going to defend my territorial right to be a slob.

Justine shrinks back a little and I see her glance at my now-empty tray, Robbie having taken it upon himself to relieve me of my chocolate pudding. I'm too beat to protest.

"What's with your old man, anyhow?" Robbie mumbles through a mouthful of my former lunch.

I shrug. "I have no clue. He used to be a decent

guy. Fairly cool. I mean, we used to even *like* each other."

"How old is he? Your dad," Justine asks out of the blue.

I frown. "Thirty-eight. Why?"

She tilts her head a little. "Well, it's none of my business or anything, but there's this thing that happens to men sometimes when they think they're getting over the hill, a mid-life crisis. It can make them go kind of crazy. My dad went through it big-time."

"What happened? What did he do?" I ask.

"You don't even want to know." Justine rolls her eyes. "But it was bad enough that he and my mom separated for eight months. And he got really weird with me and my sister. Maybe your dad's going through it, and he's got different symptoms. I mean, it has to be different with fathers and sons."

"You know, it makes sense, biologically," Mary Ellen puts in.

"Is this another fish story?" I ask.

She grins. "No, but think about it. If he feels like he's getting old, he might feel that his power's waning. And you're just getting ready to come into your prime. So he's got to flex his muscles, you know, symbolically anyway, to keep his place as the alpha male of the pack—I mean, the family."

"The alpha-who?" Robbie asks.

"The male leader. You see it with apes and wolves and other primates all the time."

I picture my father getting steamed and beating his chest while uttering a series of fierce alpha-male noises. I have to chuckle. Maybe there's something to the theory. The warning bell rings, and I realize, with a hollow feeling, that I'm going to starve for the rest of the afternoon.

Justine's got her things gathered in her arms. She shoves her chair away from the table, and drops two mini pumpernickel sandwiches on my tray. "I don't really like ham. Just toss them if you don't want them."

Not want them? I'm too busy stuffing my face to do more than grunt my gratitude at her back as it disappears in the crowd.

Nevimore the Nemesis isn't on the afternoon bus today. I figure he's probably staying after for extra-curricular activities, maybe going out for the leaping-tall-buildings-in-a-single-bound team, or some such, which he'll no doubt make, and furthermore get voted captain to boot. Phelicia wasn't aboard either, to my relief. I need to patch my tattered ego before I can face her again.

By the time I get home, I'm ready to slink up to my cave and hibernate for a few decades. Alex is sitting on the floor next to the pantry, arranging all the cans on the bottom shelf by size and color. The kid's a definite left-brainer.

"Jason, your father called from work and said to remind you he hasn't forgotten about you cleaning your room today. 'Spotless' was the word he used." Mom's voice is quietly emphatic.

I open the freezer and take out a low-fat all-natural carob-covered pistachio frozen confection.

"Jason?" The question, "Did you hear what I said?" is implicit in her tone.

I make brief eye contact, tilt my head in such

a way as to suggest acknowledgment, and murmur through the flavorless dessert. I'm vague enough to lay groundwork to claim later that the message didn't really penetrate. But I can feel my earlier resolve to stand up for myself dissolving. I just don't think I'm up for another face-off today.

Just inside my room, I drop my backpack on the only clear patch of carpet, so now the door won't close. I wade in and stir the mountain of clothes with my foot until it looks more like a range of gently eroded hills. I pick up a RingDing wrapper and two Snapple empties, scope out the wastebasket, and realize it would take a very large and possibly magical shoehorn to squeeze anything else in there. Then I think, well, bottles are recyclable anyway. So I put them back on the floor.

Depression-coated fatigue is wrapping itself around me like a cement cocoon. Despite the fact that the bed looks as if an F1 tornado made a close pass, I've never seen a sight so inviting. I collapse on top of the lumps, punch a few of them down, and close my eyes.

My head cues up a Mini-Mind-Movie, one I haven't seen before . . .

Set along the exotically wild coast of Sri Lanka, where I happen to be on assignment for National Geographic, *researching the*—I do a quick mental search for something feasible—not only am I the star, I'm director, producer, and screenwriter, too—*researching the territorial behaviors of the Sri Lankan Phooey Fish?* The Sri Lankan Phooey Fish? Yeah, that'll do.

It's dangerous to be here in monsoon season, but my superior dedication, my Pulitzer prize-winning

photojournalistic record, and my intrepid, adventur-
ous nature make me the best man for the job.

I'm reloading the film in my underwater camera,
standing there in my wet suit, getting ready for another dive on one of the most treacherous coral reefs
in the world, when I glance down the beach and my
concentration breaks . . . .

There, surrounded by cameramen and lighting
crews and makeup and hair people, is one of the top
international supermodels in the world, who coinci-
dentally happens to be an old flame of mine . . . none
other than Phelicia Nevimore! She's doing a bikini
shoot, and they have her posed in half of a giant
clamshell. . . .

Across the sand, her eyes meet mine, and there's
instant recognition, I can tell by the twinkle. She
smiles a deliciously mischievous smile and puffs out
her cheeks at me—private joke, heh heh—just as the
cameraman starts snapping away.

A rather burly cameraman. He turns with a scowl,
to see what's distracting his subject, and whadaya
know, it's old Thud. I do recall seeing the Thud byline
in a few issues of Vanity Fair, I think, as he menaces
his lens at me like a psycho-paparazzi.

I hop in my all-terrain vehicle and speed down the
beach. As I pass Thud, I floor the gas pedal, spitting
sand all over him. Slowing, I scoop Phelicia out of the
clamshell with one outstretched arm.

As we make our way toward a stand of palm trees
on the horizon, I check the rearview mirror, and note
a sudden and extremely localized monsoon has blown
in. It's churning up the waves big-time, but Thud's
too slow to make his escape, and a monster curl

*crashes down over him, then the undercurrent sweeps
him out to sea, where I see him clinging helplessly to
the clamshell, like a tiny lifeboat.*

*Maybe he'll make it . . . then I notice the peculiar
roil on the ocean's surface that signals the onset of
something ominous. The normally docile Phooey
Phish have just gone onto one of their rare pheeding
phrenzies . . .*

Several loud clomps break into the depths of my
slumber, like coconuts falling on my head. Uh-oh.
Time flies when you're in a stress-induced coma-nap.
Recalling the word "Consequences," I jump up on the
bed, causing every one of my muscles to groan, and
look around to see what small but significant task I
can perform in the next seven seconds. I start to pull
the blue putty blobs off the wall, nine down, three to
go, when Colonel Clean arrives at my doorway.

"I thought I told you this room had to be *spotless.*"

I can see immediately that the man is very tense.

"Spotless," I say brightly. I snag the last three
putty wads and mush them into the ball in my hand.
"Look, no spots! Heh-heh."

Anger vies with something else on his face—could
it be frustration? He takes a deep breath, then another, then speaks.

"Son, you're not going to get anywhere in this life
without organization. You need a system to function
efficiently. At work, we have filing systems—"

"Hey, some folks have filing systems, I have piling
systems," I say.

I can feel something rising in my esophagus, and
I think it's a primal scream along the lines of *EVERY-*

ONE JUST LEAVE ME ALOOOOOOOONE! I swallow it back down, but I can feel it sitting there swelling like one of those little gelatin capsules that grow into goofy-shaped sponges when you put them in water.

He's looking at me now with a glare fiercer than a cop's spotlight. "You think you have all the answers. It's going to be a mighty rude awakening—"

"Not as rude as the awakening from my nap," I mutter.

"That's enough of your back talk, mister!" he barks. "Just zip the lip."

Suddenly, the day's accumulation of abuse overwhelms me, and my mouth takes on a life of its own.

"The first amendment to the Constitution guarantees me the right to freedom of speech," I say.

"One more smart word out of your mouth, and you'll pay the price, mister—that's a dollar per word!"

Now my glare matches his for intensity.

Pop grits his teeth and forces his words out like a ventriloquist with lockjaw. "Let me clue you in to an important fact, Jason. The Supreme Court of this country goes to great trouble to interpret the Constitution, and certain things are *not* covered by the Bill of Rights. If you mouth off to a police officer when he stops you to say you ran a red light, he's going to write you a ticket. If you mouth off to the judge when you go to court to claim it was a yellow light, he'll throw your butt in jail for contempt of court. The first amendment does *NOT* give you the freedom to say whatever you want, whenever you want, to whomever you want!"

I bite my tongue, but not until after the words escape.

"So constitutionally speaking, I'm a loose constructionist. Sue me."

Pop stares me down. He looks like he's calculating something.

"Eighteen dollars," he says.

What? Eighteen? I'm lousy in math, but I do a quick count and only come up with nine.

He turns to leave and tries to close the door behind him, but my backpack is in the way. He kicks it and looks back at me, correctly interpreting my expression.

"I'm charging double for the smirk," he informs me casually.

When he's gone, I look at the glob of blue putty, which now has fist marks on it. I can't resist the impulse to sink my teeth into it.

Ppphhhhtttt! I spit. Putrid. Still, it seems to have taken the edge off my tension. I have a sudden moment of insight into my little brother's peculiar choices of things to chomp on.

{Chapter⁵}

The cards cascade in victory after three rounds, so despite last night's blowup with my father, I'm feeling cautiously optimistic. A delicious odor lures me down to the kitchen, practically riding on a wave of saliva. Could it be . . . bacon? A reprieve from the hospital diet? Maybe my mother's trying to jolly my father out of his ill humor.

"I'll be late tonight," Pop is telling Mom, as I close in on the breakfast table. There's a strong undercurrent of tension in his tone.

"Smells great," I say, and slide into my seat.

Mom's eyes sparkle a little as she passes over a platter of what does indeed smell like bacon, but looks like pieces of tan and burnt sienna–striped cardboard. I pick one up and it slowly folds over, flaccid as a stick of gum in a wicked heat wave.

"What kind of pig is this from?" I ask.

Mom puts her fingers to her lips, but it's too late.

Pop stops his fork, loaded with scrambled cholesterol-free egg-type curds and a scrap of the suspicious side order, halfway to his mouth.

"Margaret?" he barks. "Is this one of those New Age vegetarian anarchist take-over-the-world with tofu-power abominations?"

Busted! Mom looks so guilty, I know he's nailed it right on the head. "It's high-protein, low-sodium, zero-cholesterol, John." She hands Alex a piece and smiles, as if encouraging him to set a good example for his father. Alex sniffs it, licks it, then drops it on the floor.

"Yuch. Ptui," he pronounces cheerfully.

"Oh great," Pop mutters. "I'm supposed to eat a breakfast that even the kid who could outeat all three billy goats gruff won't have any part of."

"All right, Alex, that's enough," Mom says quickly, casting another guilty glance at Pop. She gives one last hopeful try. "It doesn't have any preservatives."

"That's because it doesn't *deserve* to be preserved," Pop says. He pushes his plate away, goes to the fridge, takes out a stick of real butter, and sits again. He trowels a thick layer of butter onto a bagel. My mother flinches as he scarfs half the bagel in one bite.

In a show of solidarity, I take the piece I'm holding, stuff it in my mouth, and grind away. It tastes like paper towels soaked with yesterday's bacon grease.

"Mmmmm," I murmur, trying to refrain from grimacing, while sending Mom an ESP message of, "You owe me *big-time* for this one."

Her grateful look tells me she gets the message.

"What time will you be home?" she asks my father now.

His gray-suited shoulders slump and he shakes his head. "Hard to say. The new King of K, S, and R has called a meeting for all us lowly worker bees. A week at the firm and already he's pulling power plays."

"What's his name?" Mom asks.

"Philip H. J. Nevimore, Junior, formerly of Dallas." Pop imitates a Southern drawl, pronouncing each word as if it burned his tongue. "I ask you, what kind of man needs *two* middle initials?" He shakes his head, muttering something that sounds like "H.J.—head jerk."

"Is he that bad, really?" Mom is asking, but my brain's gone into a stall. *Nevimore* . . .

What are the odds that more than one Philip H. J. Nevimore Anything could move to this town from Dallas, and not be related? If Thud's father is the new head honcho at Pop's firm, and if he's anything like his son, that could further explain my father's recent ugly mood swings and supersurly disposition. I feel a sudden camaraderie with Pop. We've both had our territories invaded.

"Bad?" He snorts, and bagel crumbs fly across the table. "The man's not merely a micromanager—he's a control freak. Do you know what he did? One of his first *executive directives?*"

Mom and I both shake our heads. I take note again of the dancing vein.

"He put a time clock in the office kitchen! A time clock in the kitchen! Fully grown account executives with masters' degrees are expected to punch a clock every time they want a go"—he looks at Alex and swallows—"gol-danged cup of coffee."

I raise my eyebrows. Nevimore's directive sounds pretty picayune.

"And he's installing watchdog software on every one of our computers!"

Mom looks puzzled. "To keep hackers from stealing your information?"

"No! To keep track of who goes where and when on the Internet. To make sure nobody is 'pilfering company time,' as he puts it. Next thing you know, we'll need hall passes to go to the go- gol-danged men's room."

"Doesn't Mr. Kleeberg realize that bringing his wife's brother in hasn't necessarily turned the office into one big happy family?" I ask.

"Kleeberg seems oblivious, unfortunately. Everyone in the office is already calling Nevimore 'Big Brother-in-Law.'" Pop snorts. "And that's not the worst thing," he adds darkly.

"What's the worst thing?" Mom asks cautiously.

"Softball," he spits out. "Everyone in the office has to participate on the company softball team—"

"But John, mightn't that be too rigorous with your health—"

"*Unless,*" Pop cuts in, "they have a note from their doctor, in which case they will be expected to show their support and bolster *team morale.*"

"Isn't it apparent to the other two partners that this all could be detrimental to office morale?" Mom asks. "What do they say?"

Pop shakes his head. "Sander and Roth haven't seen through the Armani suits, the smarmy charm, and the Pentium brain yet—the man's a digit wizard, I have to say. They think he's a combination of Apollo and Girdle."

"Girdle? As in Playtex?" Why would a man who reminded Pop's bosses of a lady's undergarment be so impressive?

"Kurt G-Ö-D-E-L. One of the most brilliant mathematicians of the century," Pop says dejectedly. Then his focus sharpens, zooms in on me, and oddly enough, he seems to cheer up a little. "Speaking of mathematicians, you're grounded."

The small reservoir of sympathy I'd built up for my father evaporates. I know better than to ask why. "For how long?"

"Indefinitely."

My jaw drops like a trapdoor with a broken hinge. "Indefinitely? That's not very mathematically precise."

"Jason—" Mom's eyes are blinking a yellow alert.

I swallow hard and try to be reasonable.

"Come on, Pop, even convicted felons get a specified prison term."

My father pauses to consider for a long moment, exchanging a glance with my mother in the interim. I can see her eyes suggesting a little moderation. Finally, he tilts his head.

"Fair enough. All right, let's say until the end of the marking period, pending a review of your performance. Did you start that makeup work yet? Did you do last night's homework?"

I grunt a noncommittal response, and check the clock. The bus's imminent arrival rescues me from further grilling.

"Gotta go." I push my chair back, grab my back-pack, and kiss Mom on the cheek. "Lunch money, Mom?"

"Lunch money. Ah yes, the document, please Margaret," Pop says with a peculiarly triumphant gleam in his eye.

Nervously, Mom hands me three dollars and a piece of ledger paper covered with Pop's impeccably neat handwriting.

"From now on, you'll pay for your school lunches with money that you will earn. If you're out of money, you'll have to bring cold lunch from home," he informs me.

What? I picture myself trying to choke down a leftover cold scrod sandwich on low-calorie bread. Not in this lifetime, if I can help it. I look down at the paper. One column lists debits, the other credits—or potential credits. In the debit column in bright red ink, with a note that says "back talk fine," is the sum of eighteen dollars. In the credit column, not a penny. At the bottom of the page is a small chart, with a list of chores upon which, it seems, my income is now contingent.

"Clean room weekly—$10; Wash or dry dinner dishes—$1/per—$1 bonus for both; Interactively baby-sit for Alex—$4/hour; yardwork—$3/hour; Miscellaneous errand/handy boy—to be negotiated." As I finish reading it, I drop it on the table in disgust.

"Whatever happened to the concept of an allowance?" I inquire icily.

"As a member of this family, it's high time you started making a contribution. And it's high time you learned there's no free ride in life." My father gives an emphatic, self-righteous nod. The tyranny is more than I can stomach.

"You know, you're just teed off because this new head honcho is busting your stones," I spit out. "And you're taking it out on me!"

Mom puts her head in her hands. I can tell being in the middle of the two of us is taking its toll on her, but I can't help that. Pop matches my glare. He pulls a pen out of his pocket protector, pulls the paper over to him, and adds a notation, which I can see from where I'm standing: "$22—BACK TALK FINE."

"Keep it up, Mr. Smart Mouth," he says. "You're building up quite a deficit here."

Alex suddenly pounds the table. "Gol Dang It!" he says happily.

Now Mom jumps up from the table, snatches Alex out of his booster seat, and leaves the room. Pop and I look at each other, and I catch a quick glimpse of uncertainty in his eyes, but then the stonewall facade goes up again and he starts clearing the breakfast table without another word to me. I hear the rumble of the bus, turn on my heel, and leave without another word to him.

"My life is ruined," I tell Rob as we jump aboard the bus.

"Yeah? Why, you moving to Australia?" he asks.

"Huh? Why would I be moving to Australia?"

"Bad drought there. People having a lot of trouble watering their livestock," he informs me.

"I feel for them, Rob, honestly I do, but just this very moment, I have some serious damage control of my own to worry about on the home front. Can I copy your math homework?" I pull out a notebook and a pencil, figuring on whipping it off in the fifteen minutes or so before we get to school.

"What's the matter, you run out of excuses?" Robbie grins. "How 'bout, 'Dear Mrs. Meehan, Please excuse Jason for not having his math homework. It was sucked into a black hole and now it's in a singularity with all the house keys he lost, and ninety-seven single unmatched socks.'"

"Good one," I have to admit. A shame to waste it. I briefly fill him in on Mrs. Meehan's treachery and Pop's response.

"That's terrible!" Immediately, he hands over his homework.

I stare at the paper. It looks like it went fifteen rounds with a heavyweight pencil, and lost. I turn it sideways to see if it makes any more sense. No detectable difference. This isn't going to work.

"Thanks, Rob, but I don't think a Xerox machine could copy this." I hand it back.

"Hey." He shrugs. "As long as I turn in all the work, Meehan'll slide me by with a D for effort. Why don't you try that? At least you'd pass."

"Because," I say flatly.

Rob raises an eyebrow, but he knows when not to push certain buttons. I sit there for a minute, wondering. Why don't I—or won't I—try?

It's not because I'm stupid. And I didn't always feel this way. Just like some things are an acquired taste, for me numbers have been an acquired distaste. I remember my first unpleasant run-in with them: first grade. The occasion, a special assignment, math papers to decorate the bulletin board for Parents'

Back-To-School Night, copying over all our numbers from 1 to 50, ten numbers per dotted line, all lined up neatly like ledger columns. My first one wasn't good enough, my columns too squiggly. Did I want my parents to be embarrassed in front of all the other parents by my sloppy work? Mrs. Hayes wanted to know.

Did I want that? Not on your life. The prospect petrified my first-grade heart. I did the whole thing over, stayed in at recess. I was going to make Mom and Pop the proudest parents there, go that extra mile for excellence. I put little wings and eyes on all my 2's to make them swans, little faces on all my 8's to make them snowmen, and little ornaments, with a star on the points of all my 4's, to make them Christmas trees. Suffice it to say, Mrs. Hayes didn't appreciate my decorative inspiration. Against the rules, she said, and all mathematics is based on rules. I knew right at that point I was going to have a problem with the subject.

It's not that I'm a flaming anarchist or anything. A few rules are useful for keeping law and order, I guess. But algebra's overrun with rules. And if you forget just one, even a tiny, minor one, or use it in the wrong place you're sunk, and all that effort goes to waste. It just doesn't seem like a productive use of time or energy to me.

I think of my father suddenly, always playing by all the rules his whole life, coloring by the numbers. Where has it gotten him? It's turned him into a miserable, unhealthy, gloom-ridden guy, and he's not even forty yet. That's not what I want my life to be.

I resolve not to be tyrannized by numbers or anything or anyone else.

The bus pulls up to the last stop, and the new idol of the Dexter Junior High giggly girls brigade appears, along with the Bearer of the Sacred Gene Pool, Phelicia. Today she's sporting a long pullover sweater in shades of the ripest peach over gold designer jeans, which are tucked into rhinestone-studded gold cowboy boots that look like they just two-stepped off Rodeo Drive in Beverly Hills. Since she's walking in front of her brother, she manages to send me a precious, apologetic twinkle, though she doesn't speak.

Amy's mouth goes into overdrive as soon as they're out of hearing. "I can't believe she's wearing *my* sweater!"

"What do you mean, 'your sweater'?" Debra asks.

"I mean the one I've had my eye on for three months in Body and Soul Boutique."

"My mother makes me close my eyes when we walk past that store," Debra says in a mournful voice. "She says only Rockefellers and million-dollar Lotto winners can afford to shop there."

"Well, my mother said if I earned half, she'd pay the other half. I only had thirty-five dollars to go. But now that—that—cowgirl has ruined everything."

I don't think I've ever heard Colter sound so upset. Normally, I'd find this a cause for mirth, but today, for some reason, it sparks my sympathy. Food, shelter, clothing—the essentials for survival. Amy's resources have been seriously infringed upon. Still, I have to say she'd never do that sweater the justice Phelicia does it.

"The thrill of high fashion, the agony of being out-dressed and outbudgeted," Robbie comments sympathetically.

"Shut up, Robbie," Amy snaps.

"Well, can't you still buy it?" Debra persists.

"No, I can't. They're one-of-a-kind hand knits." She lets out a sigh that could rival a wind tunnel for force.

Rob and I look at each other, and I can tell he's as absorbed as I am by this fascinating glimpse into the secret lives of girls.

"So why don't you find something even better, and buy that?" he says to Amy.

She turns like she's about to rephrase her earlier remark to him even more rudely, but then stops, as if bolstered by a thought.

"I think I will. I just will," she says, as if seized by a sense of mission. She turns back to Debra. "I just have to figure out a way to get my hands on some money. You know anybody who needs a baby-sitter?"

Cash. Colter needs cash. I do, too, but I've just been presented with the means to earn some, though my credit is overextended at the moment. Cash is a medium of exchange, to spread goods and services around. I need some services, Amy, one of the math whizzes in our class, needs some goods. Why not an exchange? I can feel the wheels in my right brain start whirring.

"Hey, Amy," I say, leaning forward in my seat, "I have a proposition for you."

"Jason Hodges, you are pond scum!" she says. "After the way you dumped me—"

"No, no," I hasten to clear this up. "A *business*

proposition. I have an opening for a math tutor. Want to apply for the job?"

"I'd rather toot a tuba than tutor you," she replies snottily.

You can't take things personally in business. "I'm talking a cash deal."

Now she looks cautiously interested. "Cash?"

"Yeah. You know, in fact, you don't even have to actually spend any time tutoring me. What I'm thinking is that I'd probably understand the homework if I could just see it all laid out by someone who knows what she's doing." A little flattery never hurts.

She catches my drift immediately. "You want to pay me to copy my homework," she states plainly.

"Shhhhh! Geez." I look around to see if anyone's overheard. Only Robbie and Debra, but they're both loyal. And fortunately, the noise level on the bus masks what could be considered a bending, if not outright breakage, of the Dexter Honor Code.

"How much?" she asks.

"Uh, a buck a day?" I say hopefully.

She shakes her head. "Three."

"That's my whole lunch money," I protest. "You want me to starve?"

"You want to flunk math and not graduate?" she counters. The girl drives a hard bargain.

"How 'bout two bucks?" I offer, thinking of homemade fake-bacon, lettuce, and tomato sandwiches. I see her considering. "Cash up front," I add.

"Okay. Deal."

"Can we start right now?"

She holds out her hand for the money, and I slip two of my three dollars out of my pocket and sneak them over the seat. She passes back her math binder, and I open it. Beautiful! All the back assignments neatly tucked in there, too.

"Hurry up," she says, and I pull out my own notebook and start to copy last night's problems. I figure I'll throw in a few small mistakes, just to ward off any suspicion on Mrs. Meehan's part.

I feel Rob's eyes on me, and glance over at him.

"Risky, Jas," is all he says.

I shrug. Sometimes life entails risks. I turn the page and a torn-off sheet of loose-leaf flutters onto my lap, with some lines scribbled on it. They're crossed out, but I can read through them.

Eyes green as jade, hair like the sun,
My heart tells me that you're the one.
You make my soul soar like a bird.
You're such a hunk, Philip the third.

Oh boy, Colter's got it worse for Thud than I do for his sister. I'm about to show it to Robbie, but concern for his finer feelings blocks the impulse, since he's got it pretty bad for Amy. I stuff it back in her binder. Besides, there's no reason to antagonize a business partner.

{Chapter⁶}

It's lunchtime, and as I nibble my cherry pie and take tiny sips from the one carton of milk I was able to afford, I'm rethinking the bargain I made. But then I think about the two weeks' of back algebra homework. If I write fast, I can probably copy one or two of those every morning, a plan I won't mention to Amy, because I know she'd put a further financial squeeze on me.

As I lick the last crumbs off my fingers, my stomach howls in protest, and my eyes lock on the feasts all around me. I look over my shoulder at Justine, who's munching on a chef's salad and homemade cheesy breadsticks. Next to her lunchbox is some kind of seven-story pastry thing with alternating layers of chocolate and vanilla custard oozing out the sides. My mouth waters. My eyes water.

As if sensing my ravenous stare, Justine turns around. I must look as hungry as I feel, because she nods at the pastry, and says, "Want my Napoleon?"

"You don't want it?" I'm incredulous, ready to leap onto the girls' table and bury my face in the frosting.

Justine shakes her head. "I don't usually eat dessert." She hands it over.

It's devoured in a heartbeat. Justine's staring at me curiously now.

"You have the best lunches in school," I say wistfully.

"Well, gourmet leftovers are one of the perks when your mother's a caterer. But she always packs too much for me to eat."

My right brain's at it again . . . A multilayered plan . . . *This has to be done delicately,* says a wicked little voice in my head. I sigh heavily.

"What's the matter? And where was your lunch today, anyhow? Did you forget your lunch money?" Justine asks.

I sigh again. "I'm on kind of an . . . austerity budget these days. My whole family is, in fact. My father didn't get his promotion, and things are pretty tight at home. That's one of the reasons he's been so hard to deal with lately."

"Well, why don't you just bring lunch then, like I do?" she asks.

"That's the other thing. Because of all the stress at work, Pop has medical problems . . ." I pause for her to absorb this, letting my expression reflect serious concern. "He's on a special, very restricted diet. We're all kind of on a diet, too, for moral support, you know? So if I'd brought lunch today, it would have been bean sprouts. And maybe a couple of ounces of raw tofu. A carrot stick." I shrug bravely.

"I'm really sorry," Justine says. "Hey, you know,

I could bring some extra until—well—until things at home get better."

I shake my head quickly, feigning distress to have burdened her with my sorrows.

"Really, Jason, my mother would just be throwing it out anyway. I mean, not that it's garbage—" she looks worried that she's embarrassing me. I don't want her to rescind the offer.

"Well, I mean, if it would be going to waste—food like that going to waste, that's—almost criminal." I catch Mary Ellen giving me a sardonic look. Maybe I'm laying it on a little too thick. "Anyhow, if it wouldn't be a lot of extra trouble, and if it'd, you know, be helpful to your mom, I'd really appreciate it."

"It's no problem. What are friends for, right?" Justine smiles at me, then blushes and gets very busy folding her plastic wrap.

A twinge of a cadlike feeling tweaks my conscience. Hey, pipe down, I tell my conscience. I'm helping Justine and her mother not waste good food.

With Amy on the payroll for math, and Justine doing volunteer catering service, I feel like I have a nice little staff to back me up. Almost like an executive. I can see why power is a desirable thing. It's very useful for getting things done—especially when you don't want to do them yourself.

Robbie's shaking his head at me, but grinning. "You're dangerous, man. I'm glad we're on the same side."

My little cloud of power goes poof a minute later, when I catch sight of Thud and Gavin Montgomery across the cafeteria. Not a surprise that these two have formed an alliance. If Gavin played basketball, he'd be a serious rival of mine, but he's first string quarterback and pitcher. Local high-school coaches are already scouting him for his dual-pronged athletic prowess. Reports are he'll bypass freshman and jay-vee teams and shoot straight for varsity next year.

Phelicia's joined the dynamic duo. I can see her laughing at something Gavin said and my heart starts an out-of-control freefall. First Philip the Thud interposed himself between me and my true love. Now I have to get by Gavin the Stud.

My mother's in a frazzled state when I arrive home that afternoon. Boxes of wrapped candles are stacked on the counter, and the table's covered with newspaper. On top of it are several twiggy circles the size of paper plates, spray painted in various pastel colors. They look like Paul Bunyan–sized Shredded Wheat Lifesavers. Next to them are bottles of paint, rolls of ribbon, and various decorative doodads like fake birds and silk wildflowers.

Alex is sitting in his booster seat, pasting random craft-scraps onto a piece of blue cardboard with a glue stick. "Bird," he says.

"New project?" I say to Mom.

"Yes, Alex, that's a bird." Mom nods at me. "For Janice Karpinski. One of the florists she deals with placed an order for spring wreaths, and Janice asked me if I could help her out. She's going to sell my candles in her shop, so I couldn't say no. But—" She holds out her hands, palms up. She looks at the clock. "I got so involved I didn't get to the grocery store and—"

"I wanna bird," Alex says. Too late, Mom and I realize that he's decided to add a tiny fake robin to his collage. It's out of his reach, so he grabs the edge of the newspaper and pulls.

Mom's mouth opens in dismay, but she's so frazzled she can't spit out any preventative words in time. Wreaths and supplies spill in a slow waterfall over the edge of the table and skid across the floor.

Alex looks down at the havoc he's just wrought, then over at Mom.

"Uh-oh," he says. "Bird fall down." His whole face scrunches up with worry.

My mother buries her face in her hands.

I'm busy calculating. "Mom, how 'bout if I take Alex to the playground for a couple of hours. That'll give you time to get sorted out here and go to the store." And give me eight bucks on the credit side of the chore ledger, I add mentally.

"Oh, Jason, would you? That would be such a help." Mom's face reappears, and I feel guilty when I see her look of gratitude.

"Come on, big guy." I scoop Alex out of the booster seat and carry him over to the sink to degunk him. I get his jacket on, bundle him into the stroller, and grab my basketball from the back porch.

The playground's four blocks away at Maple Hill, my old elementary school. It's a local after-school gathering spot. We're at the top of the slide together when a girl's voice hails us.

"Hey, Jason, hi Alex."

Mary Ellen and her little brother Nicky climb out of the wooden castle tower, cross the rope bridge, and slide down the fireman's pole, landing in the sand next to the slide. I settle Alex between my knees and we whiz down.

"You have baby-sitting duty, too?" Mary Ellen says.

"I'm not a baby," Nicky protests.

"Not a baby," Alex echoes, putting the same indignation in his tone.

"Just a figure of speech, guys." Mary Ellen smiles.

Nicky starts climbing up a stack of tires to a low platform. I watch as Alex struggles to follow him.

"It's funny how they're babies, then all of a sudden, you look at them one day and they're very small people," Mary Ellen says.

"Yeah." The realization takes me by surprise. I watch Alex reach for the next tire, miss, and take a tumble, coming up spitting sand. I make a move to rescue him, prepared to wipe away tears, but he shrugs me off, and attacks the tires again.

"Hard work, growing up." Mary Ellen chuckles.

Nicky's back down again, and he spots my basketball.

"Can we go play?" He picks it up and tries to dribble it, but it dies in the sand.

"You want to shoot some hoops?" I say to Nicky.

He nods so hard he almost shakes his head off his neck.

Alex trots over and slaps at the ball. "Hoops," he says. "Shoot the hoops."

"Won't work in the sand. Let's go over to the courts." I dust off Alex while Mary Ellen wipes Nicky's nose, and we head over to the basketball area, where a small asphalt court with little kid hoops is set up alongside the regulation one.

There's a game in progress on the big court. As we get close enough to identify individual players, I see the last person in the world I'd voluntarily choose to run into. It's Thud, with a bunch of high-school kids. And here I am, pushing a stroller with the basketball in it, and towing my baby brother.

"Oh, great. He's invaded another part of my territory," I mutter. "Okay, guys, how 'bout we go seesaw instead?" I hope to escape without being noticed.

Nicky's lip quivers in disappointment.

Alex is pounding the ball in the stroller. "Hoops. I wanna shoot the hoops."

Mary Ellen's observing sympathetically. "It's the fight-or-flight response kicking in. I don't blame you, though. Come on, guys, let's go back to the playground."

"No, wait." The flight urge suddenly turns to the fight—or at least the stay—instinct in me. The little guys want to play. I'm not going to let some Neanderthal drive me into letting them down. I pick up the ball and step out onto the little court.

"Peewee, that's about your speed, eh? Jason the Ace." The familiar surly drawl tips me off that we've been spotted. I ignore the comment, and help Nicky dribble up the court for a layup. Then I lift up Alex and assist him in a slam dunk.

"Ow!" My head's ringing from the impact of an errant pass—accidental or deliberate—from the other game. Thud retrieves the ball. I open my mouth to tell him off, but before I can speak, he bounces it off my face, then turns his back and saunters away.

My eyes are gushing a watery protest, my nose feels like it's exploded, and I'm tasting blood where my teeth just made a solid dent into my lip. Alex is tugging anxiously on my sweatshirt. I feel rage rising in me like a geyser.

"Come on, let's get out of here," Mary Ellen says in a low voice. "We've got the kids with us. Sometimes flight is the appropriate survival move."

I choke back my ire, knowing she's right, but galled to have to walk away. I've never felt like such a loser before.

When we get home, the craft disaster's all cleaned up and something that smells reasonably edible—I'm not insulting my mother's culinary skills, just her current menu—is cooking. I sniff deeply. Curry, one of my favorite flavors. I can hear the vacuum cleaner running in the other room. Not wanting to undo the domestic progress Mom's making, I sit Alex down on the floor.

"Let's get those shoes off here, buddy." I remove his sneakers carefully and dump enough sand to start a small beach into the trash, then do the same for myself. Setting both pairs aside, I wad my gritty sweat socks into a ball and put them next to the basement door, the route to the laundry room. The excursion's left me grungy, not to mention bloody. Lacking a hanky, I had to blot my lip with my T-shirt, which I pull off and drop on the socks.

Despite the encounter with Thud, I'm feeling decent. Kind of virtuous for giving Alex a good time while giving Mom a break, as well as earning a few bucks for my side of the ledger. As long as I'm on a roll, I figure I might as well go the whole nine yards.

"You wanna take a bath, Alex?"

"Bubbles!" he says, his eyes lighting up. "I wanna do bubbles."

I chuckle. "You got it, buddy, bubbles." I sneak him upstairs, thinking it'll be a nice surprise for Mom, and commence the aquatic operation.

It takes about a half an hour, but at the end, he's happy, clean, dried, and PJed. I even wipe up the bathroom floor and hang up the towels. I plan to deposit him with our defrazzled mother, then take a shower myself. We're halfway down the stairs when I hear a series of noises from the kitchen that catch me up short: a loud, muffled scraping against the back door, then a slam. A few clumsy, heavy steps and a loud yelp. A major thud and a combination of strange flaps and swooshes.

Shouts and more noises: "GOL—" Sharp thump. "DANG—" Sharp thump. "IT ALL!"

Okay, a little of the mystery's cleared up—Pop's home.

I proceed cautiously with Alex to the kitchen, secure in the knowledge that whatever's wrong, it's not my fault this time. I converge at the doorway with my mother.

Kneeling, looking like a boiler that's about to blow, is my father. Spread out on the linoleum are sheets of paper with numbers printed all over them. Lying half-squashed next to the table is a large, empty cardboard file box. On the floor next to Alex's booster chair are both my sneakers, below two new scuffmarks on the wallpaper. I wonder for a second how they got there when I left them over near the door, then it all comes together.

"John, what on earth—" Mom starts to say, but Pop's looking at me.

"It's one thing," Pop starts out in a low voice, speaking through gritted teeth, "to live like an absolute slob in your own room." The volume's rising. "But when you start spilling all over the house, causing hazards to the well-being of the rest of this family, IT'S THE LAST STRAW!" He starts to rise but falls back, his hand coming down on my T-shirt and socks. He lifts them, grimaces in disgust, and hurls them across the room. "THIS IS INTOLERABLE! WHAT THE HELL IS THE MATTER WITH YOU? DON'T YOU EVER THINK ABOUT ANYONE BUT YOURSELF?"

I'm stunned by this outburst. My ears are ringing, and I feel the injustice of the situation stinging me all over my whole body, like I'm rolling in burrs. Without a word, I hand my brother to my mother, step around my father and pick up my shoes, then walk out the back door, my own anger growing by the second.

"WHERE DO YOU THINK YOU'RE GOING, YOUNG MAN? GET BACK HERE! YOU'RE GROUNDED!"

I don't even turn around, much less answer. I'm actually afraid of what I'd say if I unleash the fury that's gorging up my throat.

It takes me five trips around the block before my heart stops pounding like a piston, and the red clears out of my field of vision. I find myself at Robbie's back door and knock before I have time to consider what reaction my shirtless, disheveled appearance might spark.

"Hey, man, what's up?" Robbie holds the door open, then stares as I step across the threshold, as if I'm something the cat's dragged in.

"Can I borrow a T-shirt?"

His eyes register slight confusion, but he shrugs agreeably and leaves the room, coming back a second later with one of his weird weather shirts. The front shows a picture of a barometer and jagged red letters that read, "Contents Under Pressure." I let out a weary little laugh when I see it, and slip it over my head.

He sees me eyeing the casserole dish of ziti and meatballs that's still on the table, along with the Pellitos' dinner dishes. "Help yourself."

He doesn't have to ask me twice. I pile a bunch on the plate he hands me and practically inhale it. All the while, he just sits there doing his homework, not saying a word. Rob can be very good company that way. When I'm done, I clear my plate, then sit back down to hang out some more. Finally, Rob smacks his book shut and jerks his head toward the living room. "Got a new video. Gonna crack it open. Come on."

I wander out behind him. Mr. Pellito looks up from the project he's working on, sanding a small antique desk by hand on newspapers that are spread out in the middle of the rug. He gives me a cheery wave.

Robbie's father is a carpenter and cabinetmaker. He's always doing some home-improvement project like this, but from what I've seen, he's a little shy on the follow-through when it comes to his own house. He'll start something, work on it meticulously, get it about halfway finished, then move on to something else. Their sunroom is half-paneled, there's a half-built bookshelf in the kitchen, there's even a half-refinished old fishing boat out in the backyard on a trailer.

"Nice desk," I say to him.

He smiles from behind his glasses. "Thanks. Picked it up at a flea market about three years ago. Been meaning to get to it."

Now Robbie's mother looks up from the paperback she's reading, a drugstore historical romance, judging from the slightly steamy illustration on the cover. She winks at me, reaches over, and tousles her husband's curly, salt-and-pepper hair like he's a toddler.

"If we're lucky, maybe it'll be finished in another thirty."

Mr. Pellito grins. "Just in time for our retirement home. But that's why you married me, honey. Because I'm so mellow, right?"

"You're so mellow, sometimes I'm afraid you're going to rot in place, sweetheart." She sasses him back with a smile, and he reaches over and pats her knee. The absence of tension in the house is as comfortable as a hammock. And the affection between Robbie's parents is so genuine and relaxed, it could almost choke me up if I were the overemotional type.

Robbie's got his new video in the VCR. I sit on the edge of the couch and he comes over and plops down next to me. "Tornado Video Classics," he says with enthusiasm.

The narrator's voice comes on over a whirling gray

cyclone that's just about to pick up a house and smash it like an egg. Some fascinating scenes of nature's impartial fury ensue. After a while, I stand.

"What's the matter? Don't you want to watch it?"

"I think my mind's been twisted enough for one day," I say. Both of his parents look at me with concern.

"Is everything okay, Jason?" Mrs. Pellito asks.

I shrug slowly. "Who knows," I say. "I better get going, I guess."

They don't ask any nosy questions. But as I'm heading for the door, Mrs. Pellito calls after me. "Door's always open. Tell your folks hello."

Back home, my mother is sitting in the living room with a book open on her lap, but she doesn't seem to have her eyes focused on the page. She looks like she has weighty things on her mind. Her eyes glance up at me, and I give her a brief wave. She gives me a small smile back, but she looks sad. As I head for the stairs, I pass the den. Pop is parked in front of the TV. A frenzied crowd is cheering as a basketball announcer describes a play with rabid excitement, and I remember, it's the NCAA playoffs: March Madness. Something tugs at me to go in and park next to my father, watch it together like we have every year since I was Alex's size. Back when me and Pop were buddies. I swallow hard, block the impulse, go up to my room, and close the door.

{Chapter⁷}

The next morning, I make a point of staying in my room, behind the door which I miraculously manage to close, until I hear my father's car actually pull out of the driveway. Once he's gone, I take a quick shower, pondering the fact that I never know where the next ambush is coming from these days.

Downstairs, Alex is glued to the tube, watching, of all things, the cable cooking channel. Mom's sorting through invoices at the kitchen table. I don't say good morning. I guess I'm feeling kind of abandoned that she didn't stick up for me last night after I bailed her out in the afternoon.

"I bought some frozen egg and sausage biscuits for you, Jason. Microwaveable," she says in a conciliatory way.

"Yummy," I say, and it comes out more sarcastically than I mean.

I hear the sigh before I glance over and see the tears glistening in her eyes.

"Sorry," I mumble. "Really, Mom. I am."

"Me, too. I feel like I'm trying so hard to support everybody, and wind up stuck in the middle, failing to make anyone happy, your father, you—" She takes a deep breath. "I really can't take much more of this constant conflict between the two of you. I did talk to him last night."

"Yeah? What'd he say?" I'm on my guard.

"He knows he's been very difficult to live with lately. He said he'll try to make an effort, if you'll meet him halfway. Will you?"

I don't answer immediately. I feel like I held my ground last night, and I don't want to regress and wind up at a disadvantage. I pull a prefabricated breakfast biscuit from the freezer, unwrap it, and nuke it.

"Be fair, Jason, please. It's not as if you haven't provoked him at times. Yesterday was an unfortunate misunderstanding. Here." Now she holds out another note.

I take a step back, not at all sure I want to be the recipient of another paternal memo. But I can't leave my mother holding the bag. With a sigh, I take the note and unfold it.

Dear Jason,

I apologize for the outburst. I'd like to try and get on the same page, here. Back talk fines are rescinded, and your base allowance is $15/week to cover school lunches. Let's try and make a fresh start. Let me know if you want my help with math and I'll make the time.

Pop

I carefully refold the note and put it in my pocket. Mom puts three dollars on the table for my lunch money, and I kiss her cheek. She smiles and seems relieved at the prospect of some family peace. Then I hear the bus screeching around the corner, and I have to run for the door.

With the truce declared on the home front, life seems easier all around. There's something to be said for avoidance of head-on conflict: It spares wear and tear on your head. True to his word, Pop's backed off the nitpicking. Of course, he hasn't been around a whole lot owing to his job. Still, I feel I'm slipping back into my normal, easygoing self.

At school, I've managed to stay out of Thud's direct line of fire. Since our confrontation at the playground, he's gone from glowering to sneering at me, but the feud doesn't seem to have contaminated his sister's attitude. If anything, she's been more friendly to me. Okay, I still see her with Gavin at lunch, but I don't detect any unquenchable spark of desire for him, on her part, anyway. And she's twinkled at me several times.

Overall, life's wrinkles seem to have smoothed out. To keep myself financially solvent, I realize I have to put in some hard time. The big-money item on the chore list is cleaning the Augean bedroom, so I tackle it after school. Five laundry-stuffed pillowcases later, I've at least cleared a path to the door. I drag them down through the kitchen. As Mom sees me coming through, she groans.

"What's the matter?" I ask. "I'm cleaning my room. See?"

She tries to smile, but it's a slightly pained smile. "Yes, I can see that, and it's wonderful, dear. I'm just envisioning being buried under that mountain of laundry."

I see her point and I feel a little bad to be adding this to her workload. I have a sudden memory of being Alex's age, before we lived in a house with our own washer and dryer, of going to the laundromat with my mother. I used to love to watch the clothes rolling around in the suds through the windows. It was my job to pour in the tiny boxes of Tide, push in the slot with all the quarters, and push the wheeled laundry carts to the folding tables while Mom steered.

"If I could drive and had my own car, I'd go to the laundromat," I say apologetically. Then a potentially lucrative thought occurs to me. I know how to use the washer and dryer. "Hey, Mom, what are the chances of adding laundry to the chore list? A couple of bucks a load maybe?"

"I think that could work," she says. "It would certainly lighten *my* load."

"Great!" As I'm going down the basement stairs, a thought occurs to me. If I can do my laundry for pay, I should be able to do my laundry, period, just to help my mother out. I suddenly feel very mercenary. Then my practical side kicks in, saying, *"What are you, stupid? Take the money."*

Back up to the room. All the trash comes out next, yielding items which would put a landfill-rodent off his food, but I'm beginning to get the hang of this room-cleaning thing. You have to break it down into subtasks.

Sports equipment goes into the closet—tricky and

potentially hazardous should I ever decide to open the closet door again, but I'm reclaiming open space. Books onto the bookshelf—some upside down, but none backwards, and most of them fit. The rest I stack in a neat pile on the floor by my desk.

The desktop . . . hmmmm . . . well, that's why God made desk drawers. I open them, preparing to do a sweep, but they are, unfortunately, occupied. If they were restaurants, they'd dangerously exceed fire-department occupancy regulations. Anything that's been in those drawers this long is obviously something I either don't need, or don't remember I need because I don't remember what it is. Where to stow it: hmmmm—well, maybe that's why God made hampers. I dump all the drawer stuff into the now-empty wicker hamper, then clean sweep the stuff on the desktop into the now-empty drawers.

It's looking better and better. I've stripped the bed, so I go and snag a clean set of sheets from the linen closet, reassemble the bed, then kick every remaining stray item underneath, where my bedspread keeps it all safely obscured. I reputty the posters. I even lug the vacuum cleaner upstairs, and by the time Pop gets home, I'm gumming up the brushwork with the debris from my carpet. I don't hear him come up the stairs, but when I push the Hoover over to the door, he's standing there, just staring.

I stare back without a word, assessing his reaction. I think it's clinical shock.

"Well," he says, shaking his head. "Well, well," he says, nodding this time. "I'm—this—good work, son. And you'll see, the organization will work in your favor."

He reaches in his pocket, pulls out a ten spot, then another five, and hands both bills to me.

"I thought I only got ten for doing my room." I feel compelled to remind him.

"Bonus." He smiles. "I'm very grateful for the effort you're making, Jason." He pats me on the shoulder, then moves on down the hall, disrobing slowly as he goes. And I'm wondering what kind of crapola Big Brother-in-Law pulled at the office today. I've never seen my father so downtrodden.

The plan's been rolling along without a hitch for almost two weeks. Thanks to Colter's "tutoring," I've handed in the homework every day, besides amassing the makeup work, which I've been collecting in a neat stack in my notebook. I'm only two days shy of finishing, just in time for the close of the marking period tomorrow.

With my rehabilitated budget from the extra chores at home, I could afford to be buying my lunches and paying Amy. But I've become addicted to something in the customized bag lunches Justine's been bringing for me, namely decent food. Crumbs from Justine's mom's catering table have not only been taking care of my lunchtime nutritional needs, they've offset the appetite-numbing effects of the Deadly Dull Diet.

Tonight, a prime example is on the table: boneless, skinless, tasteless lumps of pale poached chicken sprinkled with some green flakes that look like paint chips, plain white rice that's so sticky it could probably substitute for brick mortar, and broccoli that smells like boiled gym socks.

"It's absolutely ridiculous," Pop is saying. He's pacing the kitchen floor like a tiger with a bad case of athlete's paw. "All those extra client reports—*two weeks before tax deadline!*—just to 'bring me up to speed,' he says. I'd like to bring him up to speed—I'd like to speed him back to Dallas on a cruise missile."

"Does that mean you'll be working late the rest of the week?" Mom hands him the herbal salt substitute. He looks at it, and his shoulders slump. The bluster pours out of him in a long sigh, like a tire with a slow but lethal leak. He drops tiredly into his chair.

"Yes, that's what it means. I don't mind putting extra hours in. I expect to this time of year. But I've had it up to here with Nevimore's nonsense."

Alex sniffs his broccoli. "Yuch."

"Sweetie, those are little tiny trees," Mom tries to coax him. "And you can be the giant who eats them up."

"I'm the giant!" He chortles with glee. Then instead of eating them, he starts planting them in his rice.

"Does Mr. Nevimore ever talk about his family?" I ask casually.

Pop absent-mindedly looks across the dinner table as he spreads whipped, no-fat, fortified imitation margarine glop on a rectangular whole-grain slab with the texture of a hiking-boot sole.

"Oh yes. We've heard all about his glorious offspring. The way he talks, you'd think his son's going to be nominated to the Hall of Fame any day. He's about your age, isn't he?" Pop tunes in suddenly, giving me a sharp look. "Is he at Dexter? Do you know him?"

I nod. "Him and his sister both. They're twins. He's a prize jerk, but she's really nice."

Pop raises an eyebrow. "Really?"

He exchanges a look with my mother, and I feel like I've tipped my hand more than I want to with details of my personal life. I zero in on my broccoli and start making a little forest like Alex.

The rest of the dinner is fairly silent. As I help my mother clear the table, I take a reading on the local climate. Pop seems distracted, and not as tense as he was before dinner. It might be a good time to bring up the subject of lifting the grounding. Mom hasn't been enforcing it afternoons, anyway, and no nighttime occasion has arisen.

"So, Pop, I have a request."

"Hmmm?" He looks vaguely in my direction without a trace of what would normally be yellow-alert sensors.

I take a breath and launch the pitch I've prepared.

"I'm just about caught up with that math—"

"You are?" His eyes show the first spark of genuine pleasure I've seen in two weeks. "I *knew* you could do it if you set your mind to it. That's excellent. Excellent. And I'm proud of you."

"Yeah, well, you know. Just takes a little extra time and effort." My guilt neurons are firing double time. I squelch them in the interest of my higher cause. "Anyway, I wanted to know if I can get a reprieve from being grounded starting tomorrow night . . ."

"Something special going on?" he asks.

"Dance at school. Spring mixer." It's my golden

opportunity. I've already done my reconnaissance, and I know Phelicia Nevimore is going. No doubt her bodyguard brother will be there, too, but I'll figure out a way to work around him. I just have to make sure I get there.

"So the math problems are taken care of?" he asks.

I nod. I can truthfully say the problems, as I see them, are taken care of, and I hope he won't pursue the specifics.

"All right then. I'm glad you're back on track."

"Does that mean I can go?"

"Grounding sentence is commuted to time served." He gives me a ghost of a smile, then retreats back into his cloud of glumness.

Mom and I glance at each other, and I can see how worried she is.

"I made dessert for a special treat, John. Carob delight—it's just like real chocolate mousse."

He sighs heavily. "Sounds delicious, dear."

"Man, am I glad I haven't invested in any coastal real estate," Robbie greets me the next morning.

"Whyzzat?" I ask, pulling my notebook out of my backpack as we work toward the back of the bus.

"Global-warming trend," he reports. "If I bought on the beach now, by the time I'm old enough to move out of my parents' house into my own place, I'd need to grow gills. It's all gonna be underwater." He shakes his head.

I give him a quick grin, then go back to work.

"What did the cards say today?" He's chatty this morning.

"Didn't have time to check. Had to fold two baskets of laundry and scrub the tub." Amy's not the only one with concerns about her fashion budget. My wardrobe needs a little sprucing up, especially in light of the upcoming dance. That will be attended to with a mall run this afternoon.

I slip Amy her money and snag her binder in one smooth move that we have down pat by now, then slide into the seat behind her and Debra.

Rob gives me a look as if I've just told him I'd spent the morning practicing concertos on a nose flute. Then he shrugs and leans forward. "Hey, Amy, I'm thinking of learning how to scuba dive."

"So what?" She rolls her eyes.

"How come?" Debra can't help asking.

"So I'll be ready in case I ever invest in coastal real estate and the ocean level rises. I won't have to move."

"That is the dumbest thing I've ever heard," Amy says.

"But Robbie, can you imagine how wrinkly your fingers would be if you had to live underwater permanently?" Debra chimes in.

"Would you mind not encouraging him, Debra?" Amy says acidly.

While Rob and Debra debate the disadvantages and advantages of living underwater, such as being able to go fishing without getting out of bed, I keep scribbling away. The bus stops as I finish last night's work. Without even looking up, I sense Thud's presence with my internal radar. *Intruder alert, intruder alert, this is not a drill, repeat, this is not a drill.*

I don't look up as he passes though, because I

can't afford to engage right now, having two more makeups to get through. I flip to the back of the binder. Uh-oh. My stomach tightens into what feels like a golf ball made out of highly unstable elements. One of the assignments is three pages long. I'm never going to have enough time to finish copying it before the bus rolls into Dexter's parking lot.

Decision time. Amy's work is in pencil. Mrs. Meehan's already checked these, and there aren't any red marks because all the answers are right. Would any right-thinking person really miss a few old assignments? I give Amy the benefit of the doubt, and quietly open the steel rings. Slipping out the pages, I carefully erase her name and substitute mine.

Since I'm going to hand in the whole wad at once, I figure the chances are decent Mrs. Meehan will just check the dates to make sure everything's there. But to bump the odds in my favor, I erase and rewrite the dates. For good measure, I delete a few numbers and replace them with errors. I sit back and take a deep breath. Mission accomplished!

{Chapter⁸}

"**G**ol dang it! What happened in here?"

The next night, I'm in my room putting the final touches on my image for the dance when Pop's words reach me from the bathroom. Uh-oh. He might be talking about the mishap I had with the aftershave lotion and the bathmat. Or my exceeding of the customary ration of towels. Or the few stray toiletry items I neglected to replace. He's at my door before I can repair the damage.

"Jason, I don't want to start in on you again, but there's evidence of a major regression in the bathroom."

"Sorry. I was in a hurry. Mr. Pellito's driving us, and I don't want to be late."

He gives me a look that's stern, but not as strong as his recent judge/jailor/executioner looks, and holds up an uncapped stick of lime-scented deodorant.

"Certain basic rules have a very practical purpose,

Jason. If your little brother got ahold of this, there could be serious consequences. You know how hard your mother's tried to Alex-proof the house for safety."

I have to admit, it does look and smell like something Alex would be tempted to sample. "I see your point."

"Please go sort it out before you have to leave, all right?"

A horn honks out in the driveway.

"That's Rob and his father," I say.

Pop pauses a moment, then relents and waves me away. "All right, go ahead, have a good time. I'll mop up. This once," he emphasizes.

"Thanks, Pop." I'm gone.

As I zip through the living room, my mother smiles.

"You look terrific. Have a good time, honey." She steps over to hug me, but I intercept and give her a quick cheek peck.

"Gotta watch the hair," I explain.

"Oh yes. Absolutely." She steps back, nods, and gives me a smile that's a funny mix of nostalgia and approval.

Outside, as I slide into the front seat of Mr. Pellito's pickup, I hear a voice that sounds like an announcer with rubber vocal cords, broadcasting from the bottom of a well.

"NOAA weather radio," Rob reports. "It's a special station that gives the weather report for mariners all over the world. Gale warnings in effect from Watch Hill to Boston."

"Well, I forecast a perfect evening, locally speaking," I say. And I do. The first solitaire check I've had time for lately turned up the king of hearts, and all the other cards fell right into place like a domino chain. "It's my lucky night, I can feel it."

"You think I'm going to have any luck with Amy with Thud hanging around? She and Deb were having a big-time strategy conference at lunch." He sounds kind of depressed and tugs on the collar of his rugby shirt like it's choking him.

"Open the top button," I advise, and get ready to give him a pep talk. "Rob, you have to think like a winner. What's Thud have that you don't?"

"You mean besides looks, brains, muscles, athletic prowess, and money?" he says.

"Hmmm." I see his point. "Okay, you have to capitalize on your strengths. What are they?"

"Well, I know the mean seasonal temperatures for all fifty states, and the course of the jet stream, and—"

"Rob, weather's one of the things people talk about in conversations, but somehow I don't think that's going to do the trick at a junior-high dance."

"Well, you've always been Mr. Don Juan. What's your secret?"

My secret? I didn't know I had one. Am I holding out on myself? But when I think about it, it's true— I always have had pretty good relations with the opposite gender. Why I haven't been able to translate that yet into concrete results with Phelicia, I'm not sure.

"There's no secret," I say, trying to analyze this. "Just—be yourself. Go for it. Be bold." I'm talking to myself as much as to him, but it doesn't look like I'm getting through. I try to put it in terms he'll identify with. "If Thud's a light breeze, then go in there and be a tornado."

His eyes light up. "If he's a snow flurry, I go in and be a blizzard."

"Yeah, that's the idea. You want to make an impression."

"If he's a little local flooding, I'll be a tsunami."

Fortunately, before he can get too carried away, Mr. Pellito pulls the truck up in front of the gym doors.

"Knock 'em dead, guys. I'll be back at eleven." He gives us both a wink.

My old seventh-grade homeroom teacher, Mr. Gumble, is manning the ticket table. As we hand over three bucks apiece for tickets, he holds up a stamp for the back of our hands. "Once you're branded, there's no leaving the dance, then coming back in," he warns.

Not a problem. I'm on a mission and have no plans to duck out early.

Ironically enough, weather is the theme for the dance—April Showers. Clumps of white balloons have been hoisted up to the ceiling, looking more like bunches of gigantic albino grapes than clouds. Spilling down from them over brightly colored umbrellas is some kind of monster tinsel that's supposed to give the impression of rain. But still, it's a cheery, festive effect.

A boomy bass beat is bouncing off the cinder-block walls, and as I scope out the crowd, my eyes light on Phelicia, about ten yards away from the stage. Scanning a little farther, I see she's Thudless, at least for the moment. What was I telling Robbie? Be bold?

The DJ puts on a slow tune, which is my preferred warm-up kind of thing. There's a lot less scope for making an idiot of yourself.

"Go for it!" Robbie gives me a nudge in the back.

My feet are walking toward her before my head has given full consent. By the time I'm halfway across the gym, I feel like a lepidopterist has just let loose his whole collection of swallowtails in my gut. *Wait a minute, what's the rush?* the coward inside me starts yapping. But it's too late, she's seen me coming. She's taken a step forward! And the look on her face—could it be pleasurable anticipation?

Tonight's attire is an enticingly short dress with long, flowing sleeves, medieval maiden–style. The filmy layers of material are streaked in shades of pale purple and green, like a tie-dyed Easter egg. Her appearance is stimulating every romantic, poetic, okay, I'll admit it, sappy cornball, neuron in my brain. Phrases like *heralding the promise of spring* leap into my mind.

"Hi." She smiles.

I look behind me to make sure it's me she's smiling at. There are no other likely targets in the vicinity, so I take the plunge.

"Wanna dance?" My voice comes out a little croaky, but it's the best I can manage with my heart crowding into my throat.

She twinkles at me wordlessly, then holds out her arms, and I take a step straight into Nirvana. As her hair brushes my cheek, I catch a whiff of what smells like the dried flowers my mother keeps in a little basket on top of our toilet tank. I'm trying to keep a respectful distance between us, but she snuggles right up to me, igniting the sweat glands in my palms. Just as I'm worrying about getting perspiration prints on her silky streaks, my state of bliss is interrupted by three thumps on my shoulder, solid enough to make me wince.

Turning, I find myself nose-to-nose with Gavin Montgomery.

"May I cut in?" he addresses Phelicia suavely.

I'm about to tell him he can go cut cheese, but it's too late. She's withdrawn her medieval-maiden arms from me and aimed them at Gavin. She gives me a smiling, apologetic shrug, then turns her back on me, and I watch them sway off into the crowd.

My feet seem to have grown roots into the gym floor, and my tongue, normally my most potent weapon, has sunk to the bottom of my mouth. I'm stunned. I catch a glimpse of Thud smirking a few feet away, just as the DJ decides to heat things up with a power tune.

The mirrored disco ball overhead starts to turn, throwing out dots of colored light, which gives Thud a particularly demonic appearance. Suddenly, I'm being shoved sideways and frontways and everywhichways by what seems to be a united effort on the part of every kid in the vicinity to knock me down.

What the—Out of the blue, Justine's next to me, her feet moving in a syncopated pattern, her arms doing other stuff. I think of those cable exercise shows where a bunch of spandexed Amazons strut their aerobic stuff on palm-laden beaches.

With horror, I realize I'm trapped smack in the middle of a line dance!

"Jason, it's easy. Just follow along. It's all the same steps, then you turn, see?" Justine says as she makes a pass behind me.

I look for an escape route, but the mob has tightened into a well-drilled army of fancy-footers. As someone bumps me from the left, I shuffle my feet a little, and throw an arm up, just to avoid getting bulldozed. The whole group shifts the other way, so I shuffle back, trying to match my spastic motions to the rhythm. I'm beginning to suspect this moronic melody may hold the Guinness World Record for longest stupid song ever recorded.

"Hey, Jas, I saw Gavin cut your lunch. Too bad."

It's Robbie, to my right. I'm still stumbling, watching in amazement as he slithers and gyrates and shuffles in perfect, precise time to the music. I didn't know the man could dance!

"Where'd you learn to do this?" I wheeze, trying to stay next to him as the crowd shifts again.

"Watching *Dance Fever* when my sister had a lock on the remote. It's easy." And I have to admit he looks great.

If the Weatherman can do it, I'm determined to tough it out. With a renewed sense of purpose, I bob over to my left, anticipate the shift, and do the arm-pointing thing. Whoops. Wrong way to turn, I realize, as the back of my hand meets solid resistance—kind of warm, mildly sweaty, skinlike resistance—with a lump in the middle that feels like a nose.

Now a solid chunk of muscle and bone that feels like a fist whams into my stomach. Ooooof! This doesn't seem like part of the dance. Doubled over, I twist my neck and see the enraged face of Thud. A stripe of blood is dribbling over his upper lip, which is curled in a snarl.

Simultaneously, the DJ flips a light-show switch. The overheads go dim, and he gears up the black lights. Suddenly, every item of white apparel turns luminescent, making the crowd look like an odd assortment of glow-in-the-dark body parts. But I'm staring at Thud. Sprinkled liberally over his snarling face are a dozen glowing dots. I can't help laughing. His expression falters a little.

"What's so funny?" he growls.

"Take a look in the mirror. You have neon measles or something?"

As all the kids take note, a raucous ruckus rises.

"Hey, Nevimore, let me know what kind of zit cream you use, so I can remember not to buy it," Robbie says.

"It's okay," I manage to choke out between whoops. "We're not laughing *at* you—we're laughing *near* you."

Thud claps his hands to his face, then some primitive instinct rises up from his brain stem, and with a roar like a bull he does a combination head-butt tackle maneuver. I try for a knuckle sandwich, but only manage a glancing ear-box.

Fight! Fight! As the already chanting crowd gives way behind me, my arms flail wildly to get a purchase on something that'll keep me from going down, and I find myself with a fistful of flappy silver foil. A moment later, amid screams of dismay, we're both toppled in a tangle of streamers and albino balloons which keep popping as the umbrella spokes poke them.

The music stops. The black light goes off. The chaperones are moving in. Mr. Gumble's extracting me, and Coach Matthews has collared Thud. I look around. The carnage is incredible.

"What happened here?" Mr. Gumble says sternly.

I look at Thud. He looks at me. One message is clear—it may be war, but it's between the two of us.

"An accident, Mr. Gumble. A minor collision in the course of a line dance. Guess I better brush up a little. Heh-heh," I say.

Mr. Gumble looks at Thud for confirmation.

"Sorry," he mutters. "Didn't see him."

Mr. Gumble's not really buying, but he lets us off. "All right you two, go to opposite corners of the ring, settle down, and cool off. Another 'collision' and you're both done for the night." He and the chaperones start picking up the debris and hauling it off to the end of the bleachers.

Thud heads for the bathroom, and I make a beeline for the refreshment table.

"You okay?" Rob asks.

I nod. "That was worth the price in pain. Where's Phelicia, anyway?" I regain my focus. "Have you seen her?"

As Rob shakes his head, I spot the back of the medieval-maiden minidress, positioned right in front of the punch bowl. And she appears to have shaken off Gavin.

"Can I buy you a drink?" I say, sidling up behind her, a nanosecond before I register the fact that her hair seems to have grown back into her head a few inches and she now smells like lemonade instead of spring flowers.

"Very funny, Jason."

Amy turns and hands me a cup of fruit punch. "How do you like it? You helped pay for it." She does a slow spin.

"It's, ah . . . very special," I say, sensing the looming of another potential problem once Amy catches a glimpse of Phelicia.

"One-of-a-kind, hand-dyed, from Body and Soul," she says smugly. "I still owe my mother thirty dollars, so if you want to keep up with our . . . arrangement . . . that's fine with me," she adds in a whisper.

"Ah, sure," I say. One-of-a-kind? Someone—or some *two*—got swindled with that claim. I don't have the heart to burst her bubble.

"Hey, wait a minute," Robbie's saying with a frown. "If it's one-of-a-kind, how come—"

Before he can erupt with the revelation of the boutique betrayal, I stuff a Dunkin Munchkin in his mouth. Amy moves off, oblivious to the impending fashion disaster. A minute later, Phelicia sallies over. She's twinkling at me again.

"You looked like the Tazmanian Devil after a cola binge doing that line dance, Jason." She giggles.

I'll take that as a compliment. "You like cartoons?"

"I loooove cartoons." She drawls out the L word and I'm enchanted. I can see us curled up together on some cozy couch for an endless stretch of blissful Saturday mornings, sharing a box of Froot Loops . . .

The vision dazes me for a moment, so I don't recover quickly enough when Amy appears at my elbow.

Uh-oh. The two top she-fishes are staring at each other, and it's clear each feels her territory has been seriously breached.

"Where did you get that dress?" Amy snaps.

Phelicia's twinkle goes a little icy as she contemplates a response, but she keeps smiling. "I don't rightly remember."

Then she turns slowly, and before I know it, her forearm comes up under my elbow with a little bump, with just enough impact to send my cup of fruit punch—*red* fruit punch—out of my hand. Its contents are prevented from spilling on the floor by Amy's dress, which now has several new streaks down the front.

It's the first time I've ever seen Amy open her mouth that wide without any words spewing forth, though she does let out a few strangled sputters.

"Oh, I'm reeeeally sorry," Phelicia says.

I'm aghast. Is it possible that Phelicia would deliberately—? Nah. Even the thought seems like a betrayal, and her next words convince me I'm right.

"Please, Amy, you just bring in the dry-cleaning bill and I'll take care of it right away. I do apologize." She gives Amy a sweet smile, then leans over and whispers in my ear. "I'm going to the little girls' room to freshen up. Catch me when the music starts up again, okay, Jason?" She strolls off.

Amy's face is now pretty well color-coordinated with her dress, punch streaks and all. Debra, who's been standing next to her, takes a nervous step back, as if she doesn't want to be in the fallout zone when Amy finally manages to voice her distress. Rob, in his slightly oblivious way, is trying to be helpful.

"Hey, Amy, it's okay, I like the red. You know, it kind of—jazzes it up a little," he's saying as he grabs a wad of paper napkins and starts dabbing at her.

"Get your paws off me, you idiot!" Amy slaps the napkins away. Then she stalks off toward the bathrooms, and I say a quick prayer that Phelicia will have finished freshening up and run for cover before Amy's arrival. I'm worried for her safety.

Rob and I stand there for a minute, recovering.

"Answer: Punch line," I finally say to him.

"Don't tell me, let me guess," he comes back. "What's the shortest distance between a point inside your drink cup and a point on the front of Amy's two-of-a-kind dress? That was a pretty rotten thing for Phelicia to do, though."

"What do you mean? It was an accident. Phelicia said she was sorry."

"I heard her," Rob says. But he shakes his head slowly and skeptically.

By the last set of the evening, Amy's undergone a miraculous mood recovery. Thud's somehow wound up glued to her side, his face looking very freshly scrubbed, though a few minor blemishes are now visible. Phelicia, on the other hand, never rematerialized by my side. Every time I've tried to catch her, she's darted just out of reach. Not wanting to be totally unsuave, I've felt obligated to take a breather between each attempt to cast my net. Time's running out. It feels like something else is running out of the evening, too. The twinkle, you might say.

"How's it going?" Justine's voice sounds next to

me and Rob, as we lean against the end of the bleachers.

"It's not," Rob comments glumly. "For me, anyway. Look." The three of us watch as Thud hauls Amy out onto the dance floor. "What's he have that I don't?"

"You mean besides looks, money—" I repeat his list.

"Oh, shut up," he says grumpily. "He's a lousy dancer, anyhow."

Justine clears her throat. "So Jason, want to dance? I think this is the last song."

"Thanks, but no thanks, Justine," I say. I'm suddenly weary of the whole scene. "You saw me before—Phelicia said I looked like the Tazmanian Devil after a cola binge."

"No you didn't. You weren't that bad," she says.

I don't reply. I'm watching Gavin whisper some kind of sweet little nothing into Phelicia's ear on the other side of the gym. She giggles in response. I sigh and look at Rob, who's looking back and forth between me and Justine with an expression I can't read on his face.

"Okay, enough standing around the sidelines moping. Let's go show these turkeys how they do it on *Dance Fever*." He grabs Justine's hand and she tries to pull it back but he tugs and grins. Laughing, she goes with him.

{Chapter⁹}

Monday morning, I stare at the top of last week's retest, dumbfounded. I actually squeaked by with a passing grade, even if D+ isn't very illustrious. Maybe copying over all of Colter's A+ work snuck some algebra into my brain by osmosis.

Flipping to the last page, extra credit definitions, I check to see if Mrs. Meehan gave me any extra credit for brightening up her workday with humor.

THEOREM: The liquid thtuff your blood thells float around in.

IMAGINARY NUMBER: What you dial to make an imaginary phone call.

ADDITION PROPERTY: The spare room your folks just added on to the house.

FACTOR: An unfinished manufacturing plant.

EXPONENT: A ponent, after you erase it. ("ponent": imaginary number.)

PROPORTION: Serving size for a major league athlete.
RATIONAL NUMBER: The opposite of my allowance.
SUBSET: What happens just before dark in suburbia.

But there's only a series of red checks, no appreciative comments.

"All right, boys and girls," Mrs. Meehan is saying. "Let's go over each example. These test results were much better, but I want to make sure you understand the material before we move on to the next chapter." She nods at Thud and beams. "Philip, would you please come up and write the first problem on the board?"

"My pleasure, ma'am." Up he strolls, and I start the mini-mind-movies rolling. *The Creature from the Thud Lagoon? Nah . . . The Thud-Thing? Better . . . I've got it—Thud-Zilla! The beast from Dallas, groaning unintelligible and badly lip-synched drawls of rage, advances heavily toward Dexter Junior High School. I give the orders to the troops under my command to shackle giant chains around his paws. To a rabid rendition of a rock tune, my loyal troops yank him, marionette style, into a forced monster line dance, which leaves him weakened and bloody as a side of beef.*

Now the hero, which would be me, mans a catapult on top of the gym, and assaults the beast with a barrage of flaming basketballs. . . . He claws and squirms with agonized and vengeful shrieks, but he backs away and I scoop up the Phair Phelicia, who just happens to have phainted at my pheet, in my arms. I go through a trapdoor in the gym roof and slide down the ropes à la Tarzan—hey—it's my re-

make, I can mix heroics if I want. Outside, the phresh air revives her and she twinkles into my eyes as I snag a bike from the bike rack and we ride off into the . . . numerator? Denominator?

"Ahhh . . . simplify the complex fraction?" I repeat Mrs. Meehan's question, scanning my test paper to see if I can glean a clue as to the answer.

I can't stall any longer. "N to the X power over . . . um . . . easy with a side of hash?" I say. The class erupts in a token communal snicker, but Mrs. Meehan gives me a look I have trouble interpreting. She waits long enough for my face to go the color of a ripe McIntosh, finally tossing the question to Mary Ellen, who reels off the answer.

I lie low till the bell rings, then break for the exit, trying to squeeze out the doorway at the same time Phelicia does. But Mrs. Meehan hails me with a sharper tone than I've ever heard her use before. I have a split second of wondering if she's going to congratulate me for my noble showing of D+, but it's quickly banished as she summons Amy, too.

"Good luck," Robbie breathes sympathetically into my ear as he passes behind me.

After all the kids have filed out, Mrs. Meehan motions us to take the seats in front of her desk. She walks to the door and closes it, then comes back and stands in front of us. Picking up a familiar-looking pile of papers, she leafs through them and sets a few down on my desk. Uh-oh. I can feel Amy's eyes trained on me like torpedo scopes, intent on a seek-and-destroy mission. On the top where my name and the date appears are arrows and red question marks.

"All right." She finally speaks. "First things first.

Amy, these two homework assignments look suspiciously like your work. Do you have any idea how Jason's name got on them?"

"He obviously wrote it there," she says through gritted teeth.

"Jason, am I right in presuming that this is your handwriting?"

I squint at the papers, stalling for time till I can come up with some reasonable explanation. "It appears to be," I finally admit, wishing I could take the fifth amendment.

"And how did you come to have these papers in your possession?" she continues the interrogation.

"He must have *stolen* them from my binder!" Amy spits out.

Mrs. Meehan looks at me sternly, and my stomach sinks. "Did you?"

There's no hemming and hawing my way out of this one. "I guess I borrowed them," I mumble. "I was going to give them back."

Mrs. Meehan nods, and I can't read her expression. And I'm wondering what persuaded me that this scheme had a chance of working. Now she's eyeballing Amy pretty closely, and I can see Amy's folding a little under the spotlight.

"And did Jason *steal* the binder from you, Amy?"

I see now that she realizes there was no way I could have turned around my homework record so radically without some assistance, and she's trying to figure out just how culpable Amy might be. I look at Amy, and she's so sizzled you could fry an egg on her forehead. I wonder if she's going to hang me out to dry all alone.

"Jason asked for help with his math and I . . . I let him borrow my homework a few times. I thought he was just *checking* his." It's the closest she's going to come to confessing her part, and my guess is she does it because she feels guilty about the money.

Mrs. Meehan's nodding again, and thinking hard. She takes a deep breath, and the sigh that comes out is one of deep, personal disappointment.

"It's difficult for me to ascertain the exact degree of your participation, Amy, but it seems to me to violate the honor code. Can you tell me honestly that you are in no way an accomplice in this matter?"

Scared though she is, and obnoxious as she can be, Colter comes through with some integrity, which is more than I can say for myself. She shakes her head.

"Then I'm going to give you a failing grade for these two homework assignments, and we'll call it even."

"That'll bring my quarter grade down to an A minus which means I can't get the math prize at graduation," Amy blurts out, just now realizing what that dress actually cost her. I'm feeling doubly guilty, since the whole scheme was my idea.

"I'm sorry, Amy," Mrs. Meehan says, and she really does sound it. She marks the grade changes down in her black book, then hands the assignments to Amy. "You'll still make the high honor roll with an A minus. Better an honorable honor than a less-than-honorable math prize." She hands Amy a late pass and gestures that she's free to leave.

Shooting me a look that guarantees I'll pay for this in some painful fashion, Amy flounces out of the room. I'm left alone with Mrs. Meehan and my disgrace, which is starting to weigh more than I ever imagined it would.

I can't meet Mrs. Meehan's gaze, but I'm sensing that her mood is less anger than extreme puzzlement.

"Jason, your first two marking periods weren't what I'd call notable, but they were adequate. What's happened?"

I shrug very slowly. I'm not sure what to say. All the minor difficulties I've ever had with the subject finally snowballed into something bigger than I felt like tackling? Algebra happened? I reached a point in my life when I decided to fight back against any form of tyranny, man or math? A combination of things I guess. The thought crosses my mind that there's probably an algebraic formula to describe it.

If one-third of Jason's mental energy is used up coping with his overstressed, possibly mid-life-crisis-ridden father, and one-half is used recovering from Close Encounters of the Thud Kind, and one-fifth is used trying to find ways to avoid touching numbers with a ten-foot pole, how long will it take before Jason is a basket case, his brain is mush, and how much mush can the basket hold?

But I can't articulate all this to Mrs. Meehan. In the end, I just shrug again.

To my surprise, so does Mrs. Meehan.

"I'm not going to report you for this honor-code violation," she says finally. Her voice sounds tired, as if she feels like *she* failed at something. "You need to decide if you want to cheat your way through life. You have an F for this marking period. Unless you get at least a C plus for the final quarter, you'll fail this course."

We both know what that means—not graduating and summer school—not to mention the fallout from home, which is going to be bad enough when my report card arrives next week.

"Jason, you're a young man gifted with great imagination." My head jerks up now, and I can't anticipate where this conversation is headed. "I am going to give you one chance to salvage your situation here . . ."

She lets the offer hang in the air long enough that the suspense starts to make me itch.

"Starting next week, I'm holding a voluntary extra help and review class after school for one hour, three days a week. If you attend *every* session, and I see evidence of effort on your part, you will have a chance of a passing grade for the year." She hands me a late pass, then sits at her desk. I almost make my escape, but she catches me at the door with another condition.

"One last thing. You've shown quite an epistolary talent. I want you to put it to good use and write me one more letter."

I raise my eyebrows.

"On 'The Value of Mathematics in My Life.' " She dismisses me with a gesture, and, I could almost swear, a little twinkle of her own.

Out in the hall, I take a deep breath and assess the damage. I'm still in one piece. I'm not suspended for cheating, and it didn't sound like this incident is going to be reported to my parents in all its dirty specifics, though the upcoming report card's another issue. When I get home, I'll start preparing the field, stack the deck favorably, maybe do some chores for free, so when it comes, I'll have some extra points racked up. Amy's mad at me, but what can she really do except freeze me out? All in all, it could have been a lot worse. Right?

"How'd it go?" Rob mumbles through a mouthful of what's billed by the cafeteria as "chicken nuggets," but what looks and tastes more like deep-fried sawdust clumps. Fortunately, I have my alternative luncheon arrangements.

I slide into the chair next to him. "Could have been worse, I guess. No suspension, starting next week I have to go to math review classes after school, I have to write a letter about the value of math. I think I'll tell her it's absolute zero. Oh, and I flunk this marking period." I scan the crowd, seeking my personal caterer, and spot her and Mary Ellen coming through the double doors. My mouth's watering already.

"Won't your old man go into conniptions when your report card comes?"

"Theoretically," I admit. "But that won't be for over a week. I'll figure out something by then."

"What's on today's menu?" I ask, settling a napkin on my lap. Justine and Mary Ellen have parked themselves at the girls' table just as Amy walks by.

"Watch out, Justine," she says darkly. "He's only out for what he can get."

"What are you talking about?" Justine asks.

"I'm talking about someone who *uses* people who

do favors for him. You know why he's not buying his own lunch?"

"Because he's got problems at home, not that it's any of your business," Justine says, jumping to my defense.

"The biggest problem at Jason's house is the fact that *he* lives there. And for your information, the reason he's been sponging off you was so he could use his lunch money to pay me for extra help in math— only he ended up *stealing* my homework instead!"

"Yeah, Justine. Keep giving him freebies—if you want to be an accessory to a *crime*," Debra chimes in.

I gulp as Justine looks at me coldly. "You mean I've been bringing extra lunch every day so you could give Amy money? Your father's not sick? Or broke?"

"Well, not exactly—I mean—it's kind of a complicated story—" I'm feeling a little queasy, partly from hunger, and partly from having my less-than-noble motives exposed.

Justine shakes her head. "Go tell it to someone else," she says so quietly it makes me nervous. "I thought we were friends." She turns her back on me. I presume that means she won't be sharing the chicken salad pita pockets she's unwrapping. Sigh.

"Hungry, Jason? Why don't you go buy a phony baloney sandwich?" Amy tosses one more taunt my way, then she and Debra head over to the middle table, where the Nevimore contingent is holding court.

Thud looks up and greets Amy with a smarmy, invitational-type gesture. I see Phelicia stiffen like someone's just pumped starch under her skin. As Amy and Debra sit, she stands, picks up her tray, and looks around. She spots me, turns on a hundred-watt smile, and makes a beeline over to our table.

"Mind if I eat lunch with you? It's getting a little *crowded* over there."

Do I mind?? My head is whirling. I mumble something inarticulate. She correctly interprets it as a "by all means, join us," response.

"I really wanted to dance more with you the other night," she says now, daintily nibbling a piece of lettuce from her salad.

"Why didn't you?" Love has no pride.

She shrugs adorably. "I got tied up with Gavin. My feet still haven't recovered from being trampled. And all he talked about was baseball this and football that. What a *dud*."

So Gavin the Stud is a Dud. I grin. Thud and Dud. It's got a ring to it.

Robbie's eyeballing us. "An unexpected change in the weather, hey Jas?" he whispers.

"You never know which way the wind'll blow," I say. "The cards were with me this morning, though."

"Do you read tarot cards?" Phelicia asks, arching her blond eyebrows in surprise.

"Nah. Solitaire. If I win right away, I know it's going to be a lucky day." I daringly reach over and snag a potato chip that's fallen on the edge of her tray.

She holds out the open bag to me. "That's so cute," she says. "Hey, did you know your father works for my father?"

Her turn of the conversation catches me totally off guard. "Uh, I think he's mentioned a new guy in his office. That's your dad?"

I try to keep my tone neutral, not wanting to reveal anything about the feud that seems to be brewing between our two paternal units.

"Yep, that's Father. Will you be coming to the company picnic?" She nibbled a ridge off a chip.

"Will you be there?" I feel myself getting bolder.

She rolls her eyes. "Oh, yes. Father's orders. We'll all be there."

"Me, too, then."

"Good."

One little word—the best four-letter word I've ever heard.

"Maybe we'll get on the same side for the softball game," she adds.

Immediately my mind starts to drift into visions of Phelicia in softball shorts, me coaching her how to choke up on the bat—*whoa!!!* Better save that thought.

Rob, who's been curiously quiet, suddenly jerks his head as if to direct my attention to something behind me.

"What do you want?" Phelicia says in a tone that could be called rude, and I'm taken aback until I realize the remark isn't addressed to me, but behind me.

Turning, I fall into the shadow of a looming Thud.

"You ready?" he drawls.

"Ready for what?" I say cautiously.

"One-on-one. You and me."

An echo of David and Goliath hangs in the air. There's no mistaking: A challenge has been issued. But are we talking a duel here? Swords? Pistols?

"Amy says you said you can take me on, any day, any way," he drawls.

Oh, man! Colter's revenge—big-time touché. I catch a glimpse of her smirking over at the other table. My brain scrambles for a suitable response.

"As long as it's not a battle of wits," I hear myself say. "I never do battle with an unarmed person."

Phelicia giggles. Rob gulps. I wait. And sweat.

Thud's face darkens like a badly exposed photograph, and I can hear his jaw grind. "Hoops. Maple Hill Elementary. Friday at five." He picks up one of Rob's soggy chicken nuggets and flicks it at my face. It bounces off my chin and lands in my lap. "Unless you're chicken . . ."

Feeling Phelicia's eyes on me, I stifle a strange urge to cluck. I casually pick up the nugget. Twisting in my seat, I poise for the shot at the wastebasket fifteen feet away. It's good!

"Heh-heh. That would be one point for a *fowl* shot," I say.

"You gonna be there?"

Boy, Thud's got a one-track mind. Which seems to be focused on obliterating me. I take a deep breath.

"Yeah, I'll be there."

There's a circle of silence around the table after he saunters off. I look at Rob, who's shaking his head.

"What?" I say.

"El Niño," he says warily. "This has to be part of the El Niño event. Watch out, Jas. Could be very, very bad."

It's great to know your friends have confidence in you.

{Chapter¹⁰}

"It's not even about work anymore. It's about power," I can hear my father saying as I stroll up to the back door. He's sitting at the kitchen table with my mother, and it appears they're having another *Serious Discussion.*

"I don't understand why they can't see it, Kleeberg and the others." Mom shakes her head as she scrapes a carrot across the grater into a bowl filled with what looks like shredded cabbage. On the cutting board is the biggest peeled potato I've ever seen.

Pop shrugs his shoulders wearily. "I don't know, Margaret. Maybe the problem *is* with me. Most of the other people in the office seem to be making the adjustment. Maybe I'm just too old to change my ways."

Mom stops grating for a second and points the stubby carrot at Pop. "You are *not* old, John, although this job is certainly taking its toll on you. And didn't you say Betty Cronan quit last week? She's been Mr. Kleeberg's secretary for over twenty years. It's not just you."

They're both silent, so I see an opening.

"Hey, Pop. I thought you had to work late again this week."

Pop chuckles mirthlessly. "I escaped early. Nevimore brought in a consultant today, to do an efficiency evaluation. I told him if he thinks I'm about to work with some fresh-from-a-frat-house Nosy Parker scrutinizing my every move to see if I'm efficient enough, he can go fry ice."

"You said that?" I'm impressed.

"Gol dang right, I did." He squares his shoulders for a second, as if bolstered by the recollection, then slumps again.

"What did he say?"

"He suggested I take the afternoon to rethink my position, or I might find myself out of the ice-frying pan jumping into the fire at the unemployment line."

Wow. My father was suspended from work for mouthing off. I'm astonished. Thud's father must really be getting to Pop. Not knowing what to say, I turn my attention to my mother's culinary creation.

"Homemade coleslaw?" I inquire hopefully, ravenous from my day of fasting. "With lots of mayonnaise, as perhaps a side dish to fried chicken, hot German potato salad, and corn bread?"

Mom shoots me a reproachful glance as I catalog the items of Pop's favorite meal.

"Carrot and cabbage casserole," she says. "With grilled ground turkey patties. And that's not a potato, it's a turnip. I'm doing a nice purée."

Pop looks, if possible, even more depressed, but apparently he's surrendered to doctor's orders.

"I think Sanders is beginning to see the problems, and he's tried to referee a few altercations. But Kleeburg is the senior partner as well as being Nevimore's brother-in-law."

"So you think he's there to stay?" Mom asks.

Pop nods tiredly. "I'm afraid so." He stands, paces a few times, then opens a cabinet and starts pulling out boxes of cereal and rice, rearranging them by size and color.

Mom looks at him with concern, then starts cutting the turnip into box shapes on the cutting board.

"Hey, Pop, what do you call diced turnips?" I ask, to inject a little levity into the conversation.

"Diced turnips," he answers absently.

"No, square roots. Math joke, heh-heh. Get it?"

He looks over at me without a trace of appreciation for my humor. "Diced turnips would be cube roots, Jason. Basic geometry."

I give up. I snatch a raw carrot to tide me over and head for my room. At the doorway, a question occurs to me.

"Hey, Pop, have you heard anything about some company picnic?" I say casually.

"A week from Sunday. To *foster camaraderie*." He sighs heavily, and starts on the spice rack, turning all the jars so the labels are lined up. "I can see Nevimore there with a bullhorn, ordering us to run three-legged wind sprints."

"Are we going?" I probe. "All of us?"

"If I'm still a member of the firm, I suppose we are," he says.

Yess!! If things work out, that could almost count as my first date with Phelicia. I'm halfway up the stairs before the other half of Pop's statement registers. *If he's still a member of the firm?* This is beginning to sound *more* than serious . . .

If tension's building at work for Pop, it builds all week at school for me, too. There's the upcoming Great Basketball Battle, for one thing. Added to that is the fact that Justine hasn't said a word to me, won't even look at me, which gives me a mild guilt attack whenever I'm in the same room with her. But on the bright side, Phelicia's come over to my table twice at lunch when Thud's invited Amy to sit at theirs.

"So, is Justine still mad?" I ask Mary Ellen as we bump into each other after the last bell on Friday, jostling to get to our lockers.

"It's not that she's mad. You really hurt her feelings," Mary Ellen says. "She—" She stops talking for a second. "Never mind." She shakes her head.

"What?" I ask.

She just shakes her head again. "So, are you ready for this afternoon? Philip's been taking bets all week. Says he's going to retire on the money he makes."

"Oh, great." I toy with the idea of having my mouth sewn shut, to avoid such situations in the future. I sigh. "I guess I'm as ready as I'll ever be. Maybe I should bet against myself, so I get something out of the deal, besides getting creamed."

"He's not taking bets that he's going to beat you."

I raise my eyebrows. "Whadaya mean?"

"Well, think about it." She spins the dial on her combination lock and starts cramming things in her locker, then catching them as they fall out. I have to grin. Mary Ellen and I seem to have similar stuff-organization systems. "There'd be no way he could make money on a bet like that. Everyone would bet against you—even you, you said—so when he won, he'd have to pay out. So he'd lose if he won. I mean, he can't force people to bet *for* you, which is the only way he could win, if he won—the game, I mean."

"This sounds like algebra," I say suspiciously.

She laughs. "Well, it is, in a way. He's calculated a bunch of different odds."

"What kind of bets is he taking?"

She wrinkles her nose, thinking. "Let's see, I think it's three to one he'll keep you from scoring, four to one he'll draw blood within three minutes, five to one he'll do sufficient bodily harm for you to require medical attention—"

"Geez! Why'd I get myself into this?" I can't help groaning.

"Yeah, why did you?" Mary Ellen asks.

"You were there. What else could I say? Without looking like a total wimp in front of Phelicia?" I shrug. "I can't believe she swam out of the same gene pool as Thud."

Now she shrugs. "I think they have a lot in common."

"What do you mean?" I'm feeling defensive on Phelicia's behalf. "They're totally different, even though they're twins."

"I don't think they are. They both have egos the size of blimps, and it seems like they go out of their way to bug each other sometimes. And without thinking about who else might get dragged into their little game."

I open my mouth to defend Phelicia, but stop when I see a paper bag taped to the door of my locker. My name is printed on it in plain block letters. Detaching the bag, I read the fine print: "Don't open this till you get home."

A mystery gift?

"What's that?" Mary Ellen asks.

I feel the bag, which holds something soft. I squeeze. There's a crinkling sound. An inner alarm advises me against opening this in public. "No clue," I say, and tuck it into my backpack.

Forty-five minutes later I'm sitting on my back steps, with Robbie breathing down my neck.

"Come on, open it! Isn't the suspense killing you?"

I turn the bag over, a little apprehensively, then carefully undo the tape along the top and remove two items: a piece of pink stationery with hearts all around the borders, typed up on a color printer in red ink and a fancy font, and a pair of blue nylon gym shorts with the tag still on.

Robbie leans over my arm and reads out loud.

A SPECIAL PAIR OF PHYS ED SHORTS
TO BRING YOU REAL GOOD LUCK IN SPORTS.
ON THE ONE-ON-ONE BASKETBALL DAY,
I'LL BE THERE TO SHOUT HOORAY.
I HOPE YOU WIN
AGAINST MY TWIN.

LOVE,
PHELICIA

"Phys ed shorts?" Robbie says doubtfully. "Why not just plain old gym shorts?"

"Because the line needed the extra syllable to sound right," I say, unable to believe my eyes. She signed it *love!* She went out of her way to get me a present! She'll be there rooting for me! She wants me to beat her twin!

"Sounds like there might be some trouble in the Twindom," Robbie comments.

"Yeah, well, she's probably pretty sick of the way he tries to run her social life. And it's gotta be miserable going through life with an evil twin."

"This is kind of weird, though, Jas. I mean, I can see her saying good luck, or something, if she likes you. But buying you a special pair of *phys ed* shorts?" He sounds doubtful.

"Hey, it's a romantic thing, a favor," I tell him. "You know how medieval maidens used to cut off their sleeves and give them to knights when they did jousting and stuff? I'm going to be carrying her favor into battle." I check my watch, and my stomach suddenly contracts. "I better go get dressed."

"Okay. Just holler when you're ready." He gets up and starts to leave, then stops. "By the way, have you drawn up a will? Can I have your stereo if you don't survive?"

I glare at him, and he grins and sprints off.

Thud's dribbling a Spaulding leather indoor/outdoor on the faded asphalt when Rob and I walk up. Parked on the grass along the edges of the court are an assortment of characters who no doubt hope to go home with their pockets lined at my expense. Gavin's got a notebook and pen, taking last-minute bets. How precocious, I think, little Philip the Thud running his own bookmaking racket—his father would no doubt be proud.

The jungle gym is serving as a bleacher for some of the girls. Robbie waves to Amy, but she acts like she doesn't see him. The stage is set, I in my blue phys ed shorts and Thud in his sweats. I scan the grounds looking for my own personal cheerleader, but before I can spot Phelicia, Thud approaches.

"One-on-one to twenty-one by ones, anything behind the three-point line's worth two, winner take out," he says.

"Fine," I say.

"You wanna shoot die?"

"Fine," I repeat, and he fires the basketball at my chest like a cannonball.

I dribble back to the top of the key, turn, take the shot, and make it.

"All right!" I hear Robbie cheer as I take the ball out, mentally preparing myself. Thud's big, and he's good, but I'm fast, and I'm smart.

Okay, I'm gonna take him right to the hole on this first shot, go for a fast layup. Lightning, I psyche myself, and I'm there, but so is he, and he swats my shot, blocking it. Kids are already yelling, but it's all background noise now. Thud courts the ball while I make the mental switch to defense, but he spins and takes a foul-line jumper. It's good. Without missing a beat, he takes it out, and from behind the three-point line, launches again. Swish.

"Tighter defense, Jas," I hear. Robbie's right, so I get in close, all over him. He fakes like he's going to shoot a jump shot, and I realize too late that I'm too close, he's already at the hole, rolling another point over the rim.

Before I know it, it's Thud twelve, me zip, and I'm fighting the urge to panic. I'm giving it all I've got, including a few layers of skin off my knees. It's not enough to stop the charge of the one-man Thud brigade. Losing's one thing—this is ridiculous. But I've picked up a weakness in his game. Good as he is, he always takes the ball on the right-hand side. Thud can't go left. An ace up my sleeve, because I can.

Thud takes the ball out again. And I'm on him again, playing him left this time. He's got a whole lane open, but it's not his favored angle of attack. I force him into going in for an awkward lefty layup, and as the ball rolls off the rim, a mighty resolve bursts in my chest. He's not gonna snag the rebound. I put everything I have into a legs-up, gravity-defying, monster leap, and can almost hear the air rip as I grab the ball. Ha!

I court the ball, and my brain's racing, planning my comeback, my whole focus on the net—a layup, good, one point now—but unopposed. What's going on here? Thud's standing at the top of the key staring, still as a guano-encrusted bronze statue. A grin starts to split his face. Now he's doubled over, and it's not in pain. What the—?

As I'm trying to figure this out, I notice a breeze on my upper thighs, and a strange feeling of freedom. I look down. The blue phys ed shorts seem to have undergone some alterations. What I'd interpreted, in the heat of the moment, as the air ripping was actually my shorts splitting along every seam. What I feel is freedom from—cloth.

Thud's literally rolling on the ground laughing. He can't get up. He's wheezing, tears splattering off his face, snot pouring from his nose, completely out of control. The guffaws of the kids on the sidelines hit my ears like thunderclaps. Robbie looks at me with a friend's desperate sympathy to do something to salvage the situation.

"Hey, Nevimore, you don't finish the game, you forfeit," he shouts over.

Thud can't even speak.

Gavin crouches anxiously on the ground next to him. "Hey, Phil, what happens to all the bets if you forfeit? You didn't give us any odds on that."

Thud waves him off weakly. "I'll—pay—it's worth—it—" he manages to choke out.

It's all over, including the shouting, even though you could say I only won on a technicality. His game fell apart when my shorts fell apart. I'm lying on the ground, in abject defeat, wishing a friendly team of gravediggers would wander by and just give me a proper burial.

"Well, anyway, you did it," Rob says. "Kind of. I mean, he didn't win."

I gaze at the clouds scudding by. One of them kind of looks like a face and it pauses overhead, and I could swear it's snickering at me. Does it have a silver lining? The only possible one I can think of is that Phelicia wasn't on hand to witness her brother outrunning, outdribbling, outfaking, outscoring, out-everything-ing me. Not to mention witnessing the exposure of my Fruit of the Looms. She wasn't on hand . . . My brain's just tripped over that fact.

If Phelicia's such a big ph-an of mine, where the heck was she? I guess, though, that it's a small mercy, considering the way things turned out.

"Jas? Maybe we should get a move on—if you can move . . ." Robbie says.

"Jason, what on earth—?"

Mom looks aghast, as well she might. I've just walked into the kitchen, feeling, and I imagine looking, like I've been flattened by a steamroller, then put through a document shredder. My sweatshirt's tied around my waist, only partially covering the garment which was formerly a pair of shorts, but now resembles a blue nylon hula skirt. Blood is dribbling down my shins from the patches of raw meat that were once my knees.

"Just a little one-on-one," I say.

"It looks like you went one-on-one with a freight train," Mom snaps, but I can tell it's a worry-snap, not a mad-snap.

Alex, who's lining up his collection of miniature wheeled vehicles in straight rows on the gray mortar roads of the brick-pattern linoleum, picks a tiny train engine out of his lineup and runs it across the floor into the toe of my sneaker. "Whoowhoo! Freight train."

I gently kick it back to him.

"You got booboos," he observes, pointing to my knees.

"Big-time booboos, buddy," I agree.

My mother's turned her back and is rummaging

frantically in the pantry. As I lean on the counter, I see today's stack of unopened mail. The top envelope on the pile is addressed to The Parents of Jason Hodges. The return address is Dexter Junior High School.

Uh-oh. I stifle a groan. Things have been on a much more even keel around here lately. Pop's likely to have a thermonuclear meltdown when he sees this. And I'm too depleted of personal resources to deal with him. I snag the envelope, slipping it under my sweatshirt, figuring I'll have to figure out something later.

"Don't worry about that, Mom," I say, and make for the door as she emerges from the pantry with a bottle of peroxide and a box of mega-Band-Aids. "I'm going to take a shower."

"Well, take this with you, then." She hands over the first-aid gear, glances down at my knees, and winces.

"Just who were you playing with, anyway?" she asks.

"New kid in school."

"What's his name? I've a good mind to call his parents and—"

"Uh, I don't think you want to do that, Mom," I mumble.

"Why don't I?"

"His name's Philip H.J. Nevimore III."

"Ooohhhhhhh." She lets out a long slow breath. "Not another one."

Up in the bathroom, I set the envelope on the radiator. Then I divest myself of the good-luck used-to-be gym shorts, thinking they must have been sewn together with a very bad batch of thread. But I can't bring myself to throw them away, seeing as they're a phavor from the phair Phelicia, disastrous as they turned out to be. I fold them flag-style into a small triangle, planning to tuck them away with my personal souvenirs.

I steam myself good for a half hour, wishing shame, pain, and humiliating degradation were water-soluble. After I towel off and slip on some sweats, I gather my stuff and get ready to lapse into unconsciousness before dinner. Picking up the Dexter envelope, I see the flap is curling up a bit from the moist heat. Inspiration strikes.

Cautiously I nudge it with my fingertip, and it curls farther. Three minutes later, I've worked it open without so much as a wrinkle in the paper. Ten minutes later, back in my room, I'm resealing a slightly amended report card back inside. I'll make sure I plant it back before Pop goes through the mail pile.

{Chapter 11}

Life's gone strange on me in a way I can't quite pinpoint. For starters, I haven't won a game of solitaire in six days, not a single one, which is the longest pure losing streak I've had since I got my computer. I keep wondering if this means I'm accumulating a big wad of bad luck and when it hits, it's gonna blast me right out of the orbit of life as I know it, and send me shooting toward a black hole or something.

Monday, math review classes started after school. There are four other numerically challenged individuals in the class with me. First day, Mrs. Meehan hands each of us a quarter.

"You're paying us to be here?" I ask.

She smiles. "We're going to go over percentages today. But before we start, I'd like to suggest something to all of you. You're here because of problems understanding math. I'd like for you all to try to look at numbers in a different way during the course of these reviews." She scans the group, noting our skeptical looks.

"Try not to think of numbers as the bane of your academic existence." She goes up to the board, and draws a sideways eight. "This is the symbol for infinity, which contains all numbers." She adds a few chalk strokes, and steps away from the board. I have to laugh out loud. She's turned infinity into a little bicycle, just like I did way back in Mrs. Hughes' class. "Numbers are symbols—written vehicles carrying information. Numbers are a most useful invention for organizing certain kinds of knowledge that exist in the universe. They are meant to aid understanding, not to make the universe more inscrutable."

She hands each of us a sheet of paper divided into two columns, with HEADS at the top of one, TAILS the other. "Start flipping."

"I think she's flipped," the tall gangly girl sitting next to me mutters.

If she heard the comment, Mrs. Meehan ignores it. "Flip your coin one hundred times, and tally the results in the proper columns."

The next ten minutes are filled with the sound of skittering coins.

"All right, results on the board," Mrs. Meehan says when we're done.

My numbers are 49 heads and 51 tails. Someone else's are 51 heads, 49 tails. Two others are balanced in between the forties and the fifties. But the tall girl, whose name is Claire, is way out of whack with the rest, 83 heads and 17 tails.

"Jason, can you tell me what percentage of heads

you achieved in your hundred tosses?" Mrs. Meehan puts me right on the spot.

I look at my numbers and hazard a guess. "Uh, forty-nine percent?"

"Very good." She rewards me with a delighted smile, then goes through the other kids' numbers. "Now, repeat the coin-toss exercise, this time, doing only fifty tosses."

The second time around, my numbers are 32 heads, 18 tails.

"What is the percentage of heads this time?" she asks.

"Thirty-two percent," I say. My confidence is already increasing.

But she's shaking her head. "Percentages are calculated on a basis of one hundred."

"But we only did fifty tosses," Claire points out.

"That's right. So what would you need to do?" Mrs. Meehan waits patiently.

A lightbulb goes on in my head. "Couldn't you just double everything? I mean, if you double fifty to get a hundred, then double the other stuff, too—" I do the math in my head. "So it'd be sixty-four percent heads."

"Precisely!"

I smile modestly. "Just using my head, heh-heh." But it feels good to think I may not be a total dope.

We spend the rest of the class figuring out the percentages, graphing the results.

"Because there are two sides of the coin, the odds are two to one for or against a given side being up on a given toss. Flipping a coin is a very simple method of random number generation. But you see, a pattern emerges. For four out of five of you, your results demonstrated that for a given number of tosses, there will be a rough equivalence, half heads, half tails, verifying the two to one chances."

"What happened with mine?" Claire asks.

"If you kept flipping long enough, one tally would catch up with the other," Mrs. Meehan tells her. "In addition to working with percentages, you've accomplished something else. You've completed an exercise in compiling statistics."

"But what's the point?" a kid named Harold asks.

Mrs. Meehan smiles. "Your homework assignment is to come up with an answer to that question. What is the point of compiling statistics?"

On the long walk home, I wonder if there's a way to extrapolate the coin-flipping deal to figure out a way to win at solitaire more often and boost my luck. But the numbers start boggling my brain, so I give up.

The rest of the week is too quiet. Except for Robbie, kids seem to be steering clear of me, as if I have a social disease that might be contagious. The word's out about my great defeat—maybe they just don't want to make me feel worse. I don't know. Even Colter's laid off with the snide comments.

Friday afternoon, I'm in the school library, where our science teacher sent us to do research for reports. But I can't keep my mind focused on the task.

I give Rob a nudge. "It's been awful quiet around here, doncha think?"

He looks up from the Nature Company's book on weather. "Well, it's the library."

"I don't mean in here. I mean in general. Thud hasn't performed any thuggery. Amy's not on my case about the great math massacre. It's weird."

"Hmmm. Maybe it's like the eye of a hurricane," he says. "You know, the first wave of destruction's done, and things are calm. But the big blow isn't over yet, and there's another batch of nasty weather ahead. Better keep your head low and your storm shutters up." With that advice, he goes back to taking notes on cloud formations.

Out of the corner of my eye, I see Phelicia leave the card-catalog computer and head for the stacks. She's pretty much ignored me all week, being back on a Gavin kick. Before I know what I'm doing, my feet have carried me to the next row over from where she's browsing, then around the end of the wall of books.

And there I am, ph-ace-to-ph-ace with Phelicia. I clear my throat to say excuse me, and start to go behind her, as if I'm looking for a book, but she puts her hand on my arm. My pulse does a few backflips.

"I heard things didn't go real well for you last week," she says. "You know, with my brother." At the sound of her voice, I'm smitten all over again.

"Yeah, well, I guess some days you bite the bear, some days the bear bites you," I mumble. Then the question that's been looping around my brain for a week blurts itself out. "Where *were* you, anyway? That afternoon."

She looks surprised that I'd ask. "Shopping," she says. "I got the most adorable warm-up outfit for the picnic."

"Shopping?" I repeat stupidly. What happened to *I'll be there to shout hooray?*

"Yeah, shopping." She nods enthusiastically. "There's a fantastic sports boutique in the mall." She pauses a second, then adds helpfully, "They sell really good quality stuff. Gym shorts, too. It's kind of expensive, but maybe you should check it out. When you buy cheap stuff, a lot of time it—doesn't hold up so well, you know?"

She giggles as if she can't help herself, then walks away, leaving me standing there with my face redder than a sunburned lobster. So if she doesn't like cheap clothes, why did she buy them as a gift? I don't have to be a genius in math to know something's not adding up here.

At the end of the day, I corner Mary Ellen in the hall. She's one of the few people willing to be seen with me, and she's honest, to the best of my belief. I want to know if she's heard any scuttlebutt.

"Did you hear what happened last week? The one-on-one match with Thud?" I ask.

She looks uncomfortable, but nods.

"Did you hear anything else?"

Now she looks kind of ashamed, but she nods again.

"I know you got Amy in trouble with math, which was a lousy thing to do, but I think she went too far," she says cryptically.

"Amy? You mean goading Thud into making me an offer I couldn't refuse without looking like a total geek?" I say.

"Well, that, yeah. But I was talking about the gym

shorts." She looks down at her feet, which are shuffling nervously on the floor.

"You know about the shorts Phelicia gave me?"

"Phelicia?" Now Mary Ellen sounds confused.

"Yeah. With a good-luck note inside."

"Jason . . ."

"What?"

"Boy, love really is blind. Was the note a poem, by any chance?"

I nod. "Yeah, so?"

"Who do you know who writes dumb poems and was mad enough at you to give you a pair of gym shorts with every other stitch snipped, so the seams would split?"

It's all becoming painfully clear to me. I lean my head against a nearby locker and groan. And the signature was done on a printer. Kind of like forging a signature with a rubber stamp. The irony strikes me like a sledgehammer.

"Does Phelicia know I thought that she—" I look at Mary Ellen, expecting her to be biting her cheeks to keep from laughing, but she's not.

Mary Ellen shrugs. "I don't know. We don't really have anything to say to each other. I found out about Amy and the shorts from Justine."

I can't help snorting a bitter snort. "Justine was probably pretty happy about what happened, after the lunch thing."

Now she shakes her head as if she's disappointed in me. "You know, Jason, for a pretty smart guy, you can be really dense," she blurts out. "Why do you think Justine was bringing extra lunch for you when she thought you needed it? Why do you think she was so upset when she found out you were using it to save money to give Amy? Why do you think she tried to bail you out when you were flailing around like a broken windmill in the line dance?"

"Why?" I ask.

She rolls her eyes. "Figure it out, Sherlock."

"Just what I need in my life now," I mutter, as she bangs her locker shut and stalks off in a huff. "Another conundrum involving the psychology of women."

Something's simmering on the home front, and I don't mean one of Mom's health-food concoctions. A number of times, I've walked in on parental conversations, only to have them stop abruptly. I might think they were talking about me, except there haven't been any hairy eyeballs aimed my way. Something else is on their minds that they aren't prepared to share with their elder son.

When I get home from school Friday afternoon, Pop's car is in the driveway. Has he gotten suspended by Nevimore again? I go up the back steps and stop outside the screen door, hoping to gather some information about whatever the heck's going on. Okay, hoping to eavesdrop.

"We could convert the den into an office, John. It could work," Mom is saying in her stubborn but encouraging voice. I hold my breath. What could work?

"I don't know, Margaret. If I leave, we'll lose insurance benefits, not to mention the stability of a salary. It might take a few years to build a clientele to get my income back up to this level." Pop heaves a mammoth sigh. "We have two kids. We have a mortgage. We have—"

Mom cuts him off. "Janice Karpinski's been asking me for months if I want to work in her shop. So that would cover the health insurance. Not only would I get paid a salary, I'd have an outlet for all my crafts. And I could keep doing the fairs. Alex is three now. I can handle a part-time job outside the house."

Peeking around the corner, I see her set down a bowl of deformed-looking potato chips and a little dish of dark green dip.

"A man has to provide for his family," Pop says edgily. "And what's the matter with those potato chips?"

"That's an archaic notion," Mom says with surprising firmness. "If a man works himself to an early grave in a job that's making him absolutely miserable, how do you think his family would feel? And they're baked yam chips, which are very good for you." To emphasize her point, she picks one up and chomps on it.

Pop seems a little taken aback, and he doesn't reply.

"John, your health is suffering. Life's too short. It's just not worth it." Mom's voice sounds on the verge of weepy.

Pop's very quiet for a moment. Finally he says, "I'll give it some thought, sweetheart."

This *Serious Discussion,* which is kind of unsettling because Pop's been with Kleeburg for twelve years, seems to have ended, so I make a little noise, then go in.

"Mmmmm, what are these, yam chips? My favorite. And seaweed dip? Yum."

"It's not seaweed, it's spinach-yogurt dip, Jason." Mom still has a slight edge to her voice.

"Perfect. I yam what I yam," I say in my best Popeye imitation. I load one up and stuff it in my mouth. "Not bad, Pop. Try some. Maybe it'll help you deck Nevimore the next time he gives you grief."

Pop actually smiles at me and pats the chair next to him. I park myself.

"Jason, I know I've had a lot on my mind lately, but I don't want you to think I haven't noticed the effort you've been making."

I mumble an acknowledgment.

"To have pulled a near-failing math grade up to a B was a real accomplishment. And I want you to know I'm very proud of you."

My conscience squirms uncomfortably. I'd kind of put the doctored report card out of my mind. I would have gone for a more realistic C, but the F to B conversion was the only one that would work from a forgery standpoint. *Well, you did pull the grade up technically—with a pen and a few small alterations,* my evil alter ego tries to tell me. But even I'm not buying that from myself.

A quick subject change seems in order.

"So are we all going to the company picnic on Sunday?" I ask.

"I suppose I have to," Pop says. "But you don't."

"I have the Grange Spring Fair, Jason," Mom puts in. "But if your father has to go, I think you should, too. I'll need you to baby-sit for Alex anyway. You could do it just as easily at the picnic as here."

"No problem," I say. "Count me in, Pop." I see this as a prime Phelicia opportunity, but there's no reason to disclose that motive.

Pop actually looks a little misty-eyed. "I appreciate your support, son."

Sometimes I wish there was a way to disconnect the guilt circuits in my wiring.

{Chapter¹²}

We're on our way across town, paused at an intersection. Alex is in his car seat, following every move Pop makes with his toy steering wheel. I've never seen a kid so precise. I wonder again if that means he has a natural inclination for math and left-brain stuff. Pop hasn't said a word since we left the house. He's in a fog. I'm in kind of a Ph-og of my own, anticipating the potential delights of the afternoon.

"Go!" Alex says now. "Brrrmmmm."

"Huh?" Pop tunes back into reality for a second. He's let three cars go by.

"It's a stop sign, Pop. It isn't gonna turn green," I gently point out, as the car behind us lets loose with a long irritated blast on the horn.

"Oh. Right." He punches the gas pedal.

We pull into the parking lot and unload ourselves, the softball stuff, and the Alex gear. Though I'm eager to see if Phelicia's here yet, I keep pace with

Pop, who's trudging along like an old man, ferrying Alex on his shoulders. An early-spring weak sun is trying to make a dent in the midmorning April chill. Under a grove of budding maple trees, next to the rustic wooden Veterans' Memorial Park sign, a printed notice announces "K,S,& R PICNIC SIGN-IN."

"We have to *sign in* for a picnic?" I ask.

Pop gives me a grim smile. "Welcome to Nevimore-Nevimore-Land. Be glad we don't have to punch a time clock, to make sure we enjoy ourselves for the required length of time."

A bunch of people are clustered around the sign-in table. I recognize some as my father's business associates. Pop hands Alex over to me while he goes to complete the formalities. I scan the area for any interesting sights, the boss's daughter, for instance.

Pop comes back and silently hands me a sticky-back name tag with my name on it in Magic Marker. As he's pasting Alex's on his sweatshirt, a very large blond man dressed in a black warm-up suit with silver stripes, cross-trainers whiter than bleached snowballs, and a black ten-gallon hat comes over and slaps Pop on the back. No, don't tell me, let me guess—none other than Philip H.J. Nevimore, Junior.

"John, glad you could make it," he says in a heartily aggressive drawl. "Strong turnout, eh? Leave the cares of the workaday world behind. Is this the family? Where's the wife?" His ruddy face draws into a trace of a frown.

"She had to work today, Phil. Sends her regrets." I see Pop swallow hard, as if it galls him to have to provide an explanation to this corporate cowboy.

"Oh, that's too bad, too bad. These here your boys?"

Pop nods, not introducing us, which I guess isn't necessary anyway with the name tags.

"Barbecue's on down yonder near the picnic tables. Had some watermelons flown up special from Texas—the ones you have up here this time of year look more like limes." He winks at me. "Food first, a little relaxation, then we'll throw out the first ball of the softball season. K, S, and R's gonna donate a new trophy for the league, and I wanna make dang sure we win it. Glad y'all could be here."

"As if we had a choice," Pop mutters as The Big Thud strides away.

Normally, a getup like the one Thud's dad has on might make me choke, trying not to laugh. But the fact that he's built like a mechanical bull helps me restrain myself. I get the feeling if a joke was on anyone else, he'd yuk it up with the best of them, but if it was on him, heads would roll.

"I'm going to wander over and commiserate with the troops, Jason," Pop says.

"Go ahead. I'll watch Alex," I tell him.

As I head for the playground, I'm hailed from behind.

"Hi, Jason. Is this your little brother? He's so precious." Only one voice has this effect on me—

Phelicia's just materialized. Her pale purple designer athletic attire is ornamented with sequined flowers, and the breeze sends a waft of her lemon-meringue-pie-scented perfume my way. How could such a delicate and delightful person be related to the two gorns?

"Alex, this is Phelicia."

"Gimme five," he says agreeably, and holds out his palm, which she slaps, chuckling with delight.

The twinkle has returned! It happens to be aimed at my three-year-old brother, but I don't consider him a serious rival and as a matter of fact, he may be an asset.

"Wanna go play on the swings?" she asks.

"Sure," I say.

"I meant your brother." She sticks out her tongue. "But if you're good, you can play, too."

I don't need an engraved invitation; Phelicia sticking out her tongue at me is just fine. Alex holds out his arms and jumps from my grasp to hers. I could almost be jealous. Now she holds out her purse, a perfectly coordinated purple deal that's shaped like a bunch of leather grapes, and I take it without blinking an eye.

"So, is your, ah, brother here today?" I ask, setting her purse on a bench next to the swing set. She sits on one of the plastic swing seats and crosses her ankles. Alex throws himself stomach down over the one next to Phelicia and starts kicking up sand, while I settle for leaning against the bars.

"Yep. Over there." She points to the baseball field, where Thud and Mr. Nevimore are going over a clipboard. "He was All-State first baseman. Daddy's drafted him for the Kleeburg team."

Well, naturally. I wonder if by some chance Thud and I will wind up on the same side, or if I'll be dodging softballs aimed at my head all afternoon. Maybe I can find a way to ditch the game.

"That's all they ever talk about, Daddy and Philip.

I swear, I'm so sick of talking about sports this and sports that."

"Yeah? What *do* you like to talk about?" I can't believe it, I'm sitting here with the woman of my dreams, having an actual conversation.

"Shopping. And music. And shopping. And boys. And shopping." She giggles. "I'm a first string all-state shopper."

The mention of shopping brings back the recollection of the fraud Amy perpetrated on me, and I wonder if Phelicia knows all the dirty details, like the fact I thought *she* would actually go shopping for a gift for me. But I push it out of my mind, not wanting to contaminate this delightful interlude with the memory. I need at least the appearance of maximum confidence right now, to travel in the ph-ast lane of Phelicia's company.

"What's there to talk about with shopping?" I'll admit I'm curious. "And how do you get to be all-state?"

"Well, you have to practice a real lot."

"Oh."

She grins at me, and I grin back, but a skeptical voice inside my head is starting to ask questions. Like, is it possible such a beautiful head could be empty of any intelligent matter? I banish the thought instantly.

Alex is off the swings, rolling two of his cars along the bench's slats. Phelicia's filling me in on the perils of a Neiman Marcus holiday sale she survived and I'm trying to pay attention, but she starts losing me when she gets to the part about fashion espionage in the accessories department. Softball, even with Thud, begins to seem like not the worst alternative.

"Hey, you want to go get some eats?" I break in.

She frowns a little at the interruption.

"Ptui. Ptui."

The sound comes from behind me. I swing around. On the bench, the contents of Phelicia's grape purse are scattered on the bench and the grass underneath. Alex is holding a little lemon-shaped bottle with the top off. His lips are puckered as he alternately spits and sticks his tongue out to wipe it on his sleeve.

"Oh, no!" Phelicia and I say at the same time.

I rush over, pick him up, and squeeze his cheeks, so I can smell his breath. Definite evidence of ingestion. I snatch the bottle and look inside.

"How much was in here?" I blurt out.

"I don't know." She sounds annoyed. "I can't believe he did that—going into my purse." She clucks her tongue and bends down to retrieve her stuff.

"Do you know if this is poisonous?" I ask. Alex is starting to wail, and I'm trying to read the writing on the bottle, to see if the miraculous word *nontoxic* appears anywhere. It doesn't.

"How should I know? You're supposed to wear it, not drink it," she says. All of a sudden I feel a flash of intense annoyance. I mean, geez, how 'bout some priorities here? I'm flabbergasted by her apparent lack of concern for my little brother.

"I have to go find my father." I start jogging toward the food area with Alex.

"What's the matter?" Pop asks instantly, as I rush up to him. He's standing next to the food table, talking to another guy from the office.

"Alex drank some perfume. I don't know how much."

Pop's face goes blank for a second. Alex is bright red now, and I don't know if it's from crying or some kind of allergic reaction, or worse.

"Is there a pay phone?" I ask.

"I don't know. I don't even know if your mother's at the Grange fair yet—"

"Not to call Mom." I know the drill here. "To call Poison Control." I picture our refrigerator, and the number's right there in front of me.

"Here you go." Pop's companion, whose name tag identifies him as Jim Gombers, thrusts a cell phone into my hand. I punch out the numbers.

"Central Poison Control, may I have your name and number please?" A woman asks the automatic question. I know from previous experience they always ask this in case you get cut off, so they can call you back.

"I don't know the number, it's someone else's cell phone, but the name is Hodges."

"Would that be Alex Hodges? To whom am I speaking?"

"Yes, and this is his brother, Jason." I didn't realize we were on a first-name basis with Poison Control.

"I haven't heard from your mother in a while, Jason. Are either of your parents around?"

"My father's here. We're at a picnic."

Her voice is calm and pleasant, but brisk and efficient at the same time. "Okay, what's the problem?"

"Alex drank some perfume. Some lemony stuff. I already sniffed his breath. There's more than half a bottle left, but I don't know how much was in there to start."

"Is that him in the background crying? Is he having any trouble breathing?"

"Yes, and no—I don't think so. Not yet anyway."

"Okay, Jason, listen to me now. Do you have the name of the perfume and can you estimate how much he drank?" I hear sounds like a computer keyboard clicking in the background.

People are starting to gather around, most of them looking concerned. Mr. Nevimore, however, seems put out by this interruption of his agenda.

"It's called Eau du Citron Reve and—" I peer at the bottle. "It's a half-ounce bottle and it looks like about a third of it is gone, so at the most, he drank— a sixth of an ounce, I guess." Somewhere in the periphery of my brain, I observe that I've just performed a mathematical calculation as if it were a natural thing. A jolt of surprise registers. Then I turn my full attention back to the woman at Poison Control.

"All right, it doesn't sound like it's going to be serious—the *eau* indicates a diluted strength, and that's not a great deal. I need to know exactly how much Alex weighs now. According to our records, last time your mother called us he was twenty-five pounds, but that was eight months ago."

"Pop—how much does Alex weigh?"

Pop's looking a little helpless. "Maybe—twenty-five pounds or so?"

I shake my head. "It has to be more exact."

"Are you there, Jason?" The woman's voice comes through the phone.

"Yeah—we're not sure exactly how much he weighs—wait—" I'm looking at the little seesaw on the playground and at Mr. Nevimore's watermelons.

There are tags on them with the price per pound, and the weight. Two eleven pounders and a thirteen pounder. Five pound boxes of frozen burger patties are stacked up. "Pop, bring him over to the seesaw." I grab two of the watermelons, and Mr. Gombers, catching my drift immediately, snags the third and a few of the burger boxes.

"Good idea—we should be able to guess-timate," Mr. Gombers says.

"Now wait just a doggone minute," Mr. Nevimore huffs as we make off with the eats. "Where in the heck—"

Pop ignores him. He walks briskly over to the playground and balances Alex, who's toned his crying down to a whimper, on one side of the seesaw. Mr. Gombers and I fiddle with the melons and the boxes on the other end until we achieve a fair balance. I do the math in my head real quick.

"About thirty-two pounds," I say breathlessly into the phone. "Should we get him to a hospital?"

"That shouldn't be necessary." At the official reassurance, my whole body sags with relief. "I've looked up the product, and it's not dangerous. I'll tell you what I want you to do. First get some fresh water and a clean rag or paper towel and scrub out his mouth . . ."

While I'm taking down the directions—glass of milk, keep an eye on his breathing, call them back in four hours, if there's a problem call them right back—I hear Mr. Nevimore talking gruffly with my father.

"The boy's going to be all right?"

"It appears so," Pop says tensely as he dabs a paper towel, wet with water from the cooler, across Alex's tongue.

"Will y'all be leaving?"

"Yes, I'm afraid so." Now Pop's voice has an edge you might call a growl to it.

"Fine then, we'll talk Monday morning, in my office. You think you'll have any problem being there?" His sarcasm isn't even veiled, it's out there like a smack upside the head.

Pop looks him right in the eye. "As a matter of fact, I *will* have a problem being there. But my letter of resignation won't. Come on, Jason."

"What? Now wait just a dad-blamed minute, Hodges . . ."

When Pop doesn't bother to respond, Mr. Nevimore turns and barks at Thud. "Philip, bring that clipboard over here. We're going to have to rearrange the teams." As Thud trots up like a brown-nose lackey, I hear his father say, "Some guys just aren't team players."

I'm off the cell phone, and I hand it back to Mr. Gombers, thanking him. Then I hear a petulant whine behind me.

"Can I have my perfume back now? It's forty-five dollars an ounce, you know."

Amazing! It's like these crazy contact lenses have suddenly fallen off my eyeballs, and I'm realizing that all those twinkles aren't even fool's gold. Apparently the Nevimores are a whole family of shallow, callous, uncaring, egomaniacal creeps.

I look at Phelicia, and realize I'm still clutching the little bottle.

"Sure," I say. "It's all yours." Then I take it and hurl it toward center field.

{Chapter¹³}

Answer: self-imposed solitary confinement.

Question: What do you call it when you voluntarily stay alone in your room playing two hundred games of computer cards in a row?

Sunday night, there's a knock on my door. "May I come in, Jason?"

"Door's not locked." I take my hand off the mouse and shake out my wrist, which has mouse cramps.

"Got any spare time after school tomorrow? I'm going to need some muscles to help me move out of the office. Maybe you can ask Rob if he'd be willing to help, too." Pop looks more cheerful than I've seen him look in weeks. He sits on the edge of my bed and points. "Black eight on the red nine." I nod, but leave it for the moment.

Something's been bothering me, and the voices in my head are having a great debate. *You already got away with it—why would you rat yourself out?* one of them says. *You've gotten away with a lot,* a different one comments. *And where has it gotten you?* I'm not sure about the answer to that one. *Besides, you're going to have to do a repeat performance of doctoring the last report card of the year when it arrives, or the deception'll come out anyway,* a third one chimes in. *Shut up,* I tell them all. *Wouldya let me think a minute?*

All the way home from the park, Pop was telling me how proud he was of me for the way I handled things with Alex. He recapped it for Mom over dinner, never once mentioning the fact that if I'd been watching him more closely, it wouldn't have happened. Right now something in me is feeling like I'm violating some internal honor code I didn't even realize I had, by letting him believe I've been rehabilitated.

I look at the computer. This game's a goner, I can tell already. With solitaire, sometimes the cards fall right into place. Sometimes you really have to work 'em, bring cards you've already stacked on the aces down in order to whittle away at the pile, and in the end, it comes out okay. Other times, it looks like everything's peeling off perfectly, but you come up against a gridlock, and you can't go anywhere. And sometimes you're just stuck with a lousy deal, and no matter what you do, you're not gonna win. Then you fold. Knowing when to cut your losses is not a bad thing.

"I can help you late in the afternoon," I say. "But I have to stay after school for a special math review class."

He beams at me, and I can see he's getting ready

to go into proud-Pop mode again, but I head him off at the pass. Somehow, according to this newly awakened code in me, the loss I need to cut now is one that goes with him thinking I'm better than I am, when I don't deserve it. I don't know what the price is going to be, but I have to do it.

"Pop, I have to go, because I flunked math this marking period. It's my only shot at passing for the year."

He's looking puzzled. "Your report card said you had a B. And I thought you made up all the work."

I take a deep breath and sketch the sordid details for him, then wait for him to announce his verdict and my sentence. I feel bad, but somehow, I also feel good.

"All right," he finally says after a long silence, and stands up. "How does 4:30 sound? Will you be home by then?"

"Yeah, I should be." I'm still waiting for the ax to fall. "That's it? I mean, don't I get grounded? Or fined? Or disowned?"

He goes over to the door, puts a hand on the knob, then looks back at me, giving a nod to the computer screen.

"Some things in life are solitary endeavors. Personal integrity is one of them," he says quietly. "There's not always an obvious payoff. In fact, sometimes it seems like you're losing. But one thing I've learned, and maybe you're learning it, too. You have to be able to live with yourself. If you want to be reasonably happy, you better make yourself into someone that you want to live with." He leaves.

I look back at the computer and X out my current game, leaving the window with the scorecard I've been keeping open. I look at the list of times, and points and wins and losses, a collection of seemingly random numbers, and wonder if there's any meaning, any pattern, anything that'll give me a clue. I pull up the calculator program and start fooling around.

"What's the forecast?" I ask Rob at the bus stop the next morning.

"Tropical depression brewing in the south Atlantic." He shrugs. "Wonder if they'll name the first hurricane of the year 'Amy.'" He grins a wry grin.

"I think I'll e-mail the National Storm Tracking Center and tell them they should jump straight to Phelicia. A big mass of hot air from the south."

He raises his eyebrows. "What made you see the light? I was wondering how long it was going to take."

I fill him in on the picnic.

"You think the feud with Thud's over?"

I shrug. I'm thinking back to what Mary Ellen said about survival of the fittest and the primitive "fight or flight," and the fact that there are times when "flight" is the appropriate survival move. Maybe I'm more like Pop than I realized. I really admire him for quitting.

"Nothing to fight about anymore, as far as his sister goes."

"You mean, there are other P-H-ish in the sea?" Rob cracks.

It's lunchtime, and I'm munching on two genuine, austerity-plan, homemade peanut butter and jellies.

Pop and Mom laid out the budget numbers last night, and we won't be going on any Caribbean cruises for a while.

I catch Justine eyeing my Spartan fare as she opens a plastic container of pasta salad, and sets aside a piece of what looks like Toll House cookie pie. I give her a little smile, just a quick one. She looks away. I drop my own eyes and concentrate on the holes in my Wonder Bread.

Phelicia, decked out with her usual ph-lair, is chatting up Gavin. I check my galvanic skin response, and my pulse cautiously. *Nada.* The ph-ever's gone—I'm cured. Gavin looks like he's starting to glaze over at the conversation, and I can't help smirking.

"Here." A piece of Toll House cookie pie lands gently on my tray. "I'm not going to eat it anyway."

Justine's on her way out before I can say thanks. I feel the sudden need to make some amends, so I jump up and trot after her.

"Hey, Justine."

She turns around, her eyebrows raised slightly, and waits.

"Listen, I'm sorry about—well, you know, everything. And thanks. A lot. For the pie and all. And— I was just thinking, I know it's a ways away, but the graduation dance—do you want to, well, maybe go together? You, with me?"

A nice, warm feeling, kind of righteous and generous, spreads through me, sparked by Justine's surprised and pleased expression. Then her look shifts to one of friendly regret.

"Thanks, Jason, but I've kind of already committed to going with someone."

Oh?

"Who?" I ask bluntly.

She looks down at her shoes, smiles a little sheepishly, then looks up. And now *she's* doing that girl-twinkle thing as she points to Robbie, who's just sidled up next to us. Geez! I'm astonished. But—not unhappy. Just—I don't know. In the end I just grin and clap him on the shoulder. He shrugs, grins back, does a little dance step, and the two of them head off to class.

Dear Mrs. Meehan,

I know all the obvious reasons why math has some worth to it. You have to be able to keep track of monetary affairs. If you're a pilot, you need to know about math so you can keep your plane up in the air. If you're an athlete, keeping track of your stats lets you know if you're doing your job well enough, or what an opponent's weaknesses might be. If you're a meteorologist, you can use data to give people important information, like a tornado's likely to head your way, so take cover. Or if your little brother has a habit of ingesting potentially harmful substances, a little math knowledge can help you assist Poison Control in making an over-the-phone diagnosis.

I can see the value of math in life, really. It's practical stuff. That doesn't make algebra any easier for me, somehow.

I kept a record of my computer solitaire stats for two hundred games this weekend. Here they are:

	POINTS	TIME (seconds)	CARDS UP	GAMES PLAYED
Losses:	17,680	13,168	704	176
Wins:	109,152	4,296	1,248	24

I read somewhere that the standard odds in solitaire are winning one game out of thirty. Dividing 30 into 1, that works out to being lucky about 3% of the time. So out of 200 games, I could have counted on winning maybe 6 games.

Adding up my points scored for both wins and losses, out of a total of 126,832 points, 14% of them were earned in games that I lost, while 86% of them were earned in games that I won. So a lot of the effort expended didn't yield much, but when I won, the results were big-time wins that more than made up for the losses.

Furthermore adding up the time spent, a total of 17,464 seconds, or about 292 minutes, I spent 75% of the time on losing games, again not getting anywhere for the effort, and only 25% of the time winning.

Finally out of 200 games played, I won 12% of them, and lost 88% of them, which seems to be pretty good according to what could be expected from standard odds.

Of course, there may be things built into computer decks that I don't know about so I haven't factored them in. It probably involves more advanced calculations than I'm ready to tackle.

But as close as I can figure, my results show that I'm a fairly lucky guy, on average. Looking at the numbers, I guess I spent a lot more time losing than winning, but when I won, the bonus points made the wins big, point-wise. What else does it mean? If on a really lucky day, a guy's luck is running 12%, I guess it means he's going to need to rely on something other than luck for the other 88%. Like maybe his own efforts?

I think I'm going to lay off the solitaire. I've decided it's a little too linear and confining for the right half of my brain. I found a new game though, called Free Cell, which I think suits my free spirit better. Plus, they say it's theoretically possible to win every game. Got to like those odds!

Anyhow, I want to say thanks for putting up with me, for giving me a second (okay, and a third and a fourth) chance, and most of all, for teaching me something even more important than algebra.

Jason "The Ace" Hodges